Tiger in a Cage

Tiger in a Cage

THE MEMOIR OF WU TEK YING

吴悌音

Alma Wu

Betty Orbach

Carol W. Hazelwood

Copyright © 2000 by Alma Wu, Betty Orbach, and Carol W. Hazelwood.

Library of Congress Number: 00-192769
ISBN #: Hardcover 0-7388-4813-1
Softcover 0-7388-4814-X

All rights reserved. No part of this book may be reproduced or transmitted in any form or by any means, electronic or mechanical, including photocopying, recording, or by any information storage and retrieval system, without permission in writing from the copyright owner.

This book was printed in the United States of America.

To order additional copies of this book, contact:
Xlibris Corporation
1-888-7-XLIBRIS
www.Xlibris.com
Orders@Xlibris.com

Contents

LIST OF MAIN CHARACTERS	9
HISTORICAL TIMEFRAME	11
CHAPTER 1	15
CHAPTER 2	24
CHAPTER 3	42
CHAPTER 4	55
CHAPTER 5	61
CHAPTER 6	76
CHAPTER 7	84
CHAPTER 8	91
CHAPTER 9	98
CHAPTER 10	104
CHAPTER 11	109
CHAPTER 12	115
CHAPTER 13	118
CHAPTER 14	127
CHAPTER 15	131
CHAPTER 16	137
CHAPTER 17	142
CHAPTER 18	148
CHAPTER 19	154
CHAPTER 20	162
CHAPTER 21	171
CHAPTER 22	182
CHAPTER 23	191
CHAPTER 24	198
CHAPTER 25	206
CHAPTER 26	214

CHAPTER 27	219
CHAPTER 28	227
CHAPTER 29	234
EPILOGUE	243

Tiger in a Cage is dedicated in loving memory to Tek Ying's father, Wu Pei Ching, and Tek Ying's eldest daughter, Teresa.

WU TEK YING

List of Main Characters

Tek Ying—Alma Wu
Wu Pei Ching—Tek Ying's father
Sau Yuk—Tek Ying's mother
Pun Yun—Second wife to Pei Ching
Sio Ying—Pei Ching's mistress
Gun Yuen—Son of Pei Ching and Sio Ying
U-Ching—Accepted son of Pei Ching and Sau Yuk
Shiu Ching—Son of Pei Ching and Pun Yun
Tsu Ching—Second son of Pei Ching and Pun Yun
Sun Mei—Daughter of Pei Ching and Sau Yuk
Wong Yen Tai—Pei Ching's friend
Wong Hai Li—Yen Tai's wife
Auntie Yuk Ching—Pei Ching's sister
Lok Hsiao-ming—Manager of Wu land in Wu Sih
Spring Orchid—Ya Tua—slave girl
Eddie Lamb—Tek Ying's first husband
Lee Chou—Tek Ying's second husband
Sidney—Tek Ying's first boyfriend
Illan Kwok—Tek Ying's high school friend
Lucy To—Tek Ying's friend
Maria—Tek Ying's friend
Vera—Tek Ying's friend

Historical Timeframe

The Wu family's lives and fortunes were intricately linked to the unraveling of China's cultural and economic history during China's turbulent years of 1914–1952. Tek Ying was born in Shantung Province where her father worked under the famous warlord, Zhang Zoulin. With Zhang's murder by the Japanese, the now well-to-do Wu family moved to Shanghia and built a home in the French Concession.

The French Concession and the International Settlement came into existence as a result of China's defeat in the Opium Wars in 1842. China conceded privileges to Russia, Japan, England, France, Holland and the United States by permitting these nations to establish free ports. Shanghai was designated a free port, and its officials maintained a minimum of trade regulations. China became a cage, with port cities like Shanghai, its gateways to the world. Foreign powers ruled Shanghai's International Settlement and the French Concession, but while these foreign concessions were physically and politically separate from the Chinese sections, Chinese had lived there for years. They had built homes, continued to respect old customs and attempted to maintain their culture.

In time the wave of western thought, architecture and culture made inroads into every aspect of the lives of the Chinese. China of the early 1900s underwent major upheavals: foreign intervention, political unrest, revolution and an enigmatic quest for religious balance. News reporting, broadened by outside contact, widened China's view of the world. Western dress influenced military uniforms, and the western business suit supplemented the traditional Chinese gown. Changes took place in the educational system; students, who had worn queues to show obedience to the emperor, cut off their queues. Protestant missionaries crusaded against foot binding and opium smoking. It was a time of shedding the past, a time of interweaving new threads into an old tapestry. Traditions then were challenged, yet China's culture remained of a piece—its charm and its failure.

The Japanese military flexed its might when it took over Manchuria in 1931. The Chinese Nationalist and Communist armies fought the Japanese as well as each other. In 1937 the Japanese seized Shanghai and irrevocably altered the most uniquely international city of the 1920s and 1930s. The city never recovered, but although war swirled around Shanghai, the International Settlement and the French Concession remained relatively free from war from 1927 until 1943. Foreigners, as well as Chinese, sought protection inside the foreign enclaves, and the Chinese remained insulated from much of what was happening in the rest of China.

After the Japanese occupation ended, Chiang Kaishek's government took control of Shanghai, wielding power with venal corruption and draining wealth from the people. When the Communists took over Shanghai in 1949, the city lacked its former vitality. What individuality, wealth and family resources survived, the Communists destroyed. Shanghai had withstood the Japanese and Chiang Kaishek's Guomindang, but it was Communism that struck the final blow against tradition. Families were divided, homes destroyed or taken over by government officials and customs shredded. The old culture was shattered and nothing replaced it. Communism swallowed the Chinese into a new cage.

TIGER IN A CAGE is the memoir of Wu Tek Ying, as she relates the rise and fall of her tradition-bound family, dominated by her father.

Chapter 1

1914–1916

It was evening. The flickering light from oil lamps encased three generations of Wu men in light and shadows. Seventeen-year-old Pei Ching, arms stiff at his side, stood facing his seated grandfather. The nails of Pei Ching's clenched fingers drew blood from his palms. "Yei, Yei," he began, then faltered. "Yei, Yei, I respectfully ask you to help me get a job at the Longhua Arsenal where you work."

Silence met that request. His grandfather turned to stare at Pei Ching's father, who sat on a wooden stool in a shadowed corner. "You," he pointed to his opium-drugged son, "are responsible for your son. You have thrown away your future. Once you were a scholar. Look at you now. You disgrace the family!"

Pei Ching's father nodded, too drugged from opium to think properly, and blinked with glassy eyes. The brown-stained fingers of his trembling hand lifted a cigarette to his mouth, and he inhaled.

"I don't wish to cause trouble, Yei Yei." Pei Ching protested. "Father doesn't have the forty yuan I need for the YMCA school. I understand that. I must get a job."

The grandfather nodded and peered through his small, round glasses at the tall, handsome boy. "I don't like what I see of the past. I gave your father everything. Look at him!" His voice quivered. "A scholar no more. A heap of skin around an empty skull."

The grandfather rose, his gray gown trailing from his thin frame. His half-closed eyes appeared to be imagining a different version of his sulking son. Again he pointed at Pei Ching's father, who raised his tar stained hands to shield his face from the wrath of the older man. "I've had enough of your behavior," the old man said. "You leave your son penniless. If you don't rid yourself of your opium habit, your life here in Shanghai is ended. Do you understand? You will return to Wu Sih to be with your wife. You will be thrust out of my house."

He turned back to Pei Ching. "I will not help you get a job at the arsenal. You must do this on your own. But you have been a filial son and may remain in my house. You are strong. Stay strong!"

Pei Ching bowed slightly and stepped away from his grandfather. His head swarmed with hope and frustration. Alone in the next room he stood very still, threw back his shoulders; his eyes steadied.

The following week he passed the test to work on the lathe at the factory and at the age of seventeen became a mechanic at the arsenal. The factory issued him one blue uniform. Every night he washed it and rose at four in the morning to hold it over a bowl of steaming water to smooth out the wrinkles. His daily neat appearance impressed his fellow factory workers. Why did he have several uniforms, and they only one?

Pei Ching worked full days, week after week, but was

unable to save money. At each pay period his father asked for Pei Ching's wages and used them for his opium habit. Despite the grandfather's recriminations toward his son, nothing changed. Family ties were chains not easily removed and first sons were spoiled. Pei Ching's loyalty to his father forbade a confrontation, and the Wu home in Shanghai became less a sanctuary and more a cage.

After Pei Ching's grandmother died, his grandfather remarried. This woman was the third wife of a widower. She brought Sio Ying, the beautiful daughter of the widower's second wife, with her to the marriage. According to Chinese culture, Sio Ying became Pei Ching's aunt with all the taboos of a blood relationship. She was two years older than Pei Ching, beautiful, seductive and irresistible to Pei Ching. Living in the same house, the inevitable happened. They fell in love.

One morning while the rest of the house slept, Sio Ying wakened early to catch Pei Ching as he worked in the dark kitchen steaming his uniform free of wrinkles. She stood in the shadows, unsure of the way to tell her young lover her troubling news. Upon noticing her, he smiled and nodded to her, but continued his task.

Sio Ying minced forward on her tiny half-bound feet. Waiting, wanting to speak, yet fearing Pei Ching's reaction, she at last blurted out, "I have brought great sorrow to my family because of my love for you." Tears brimmed Sio Ying's dark eyes. She slid her small graceful hands down the front of her gown. "I'm with child. What will I do?"

Pei Ching's face flushed. He looked up at her through the steam curling around his face. This possibility had not occurred to him. He was mortified that their secret love would now be discovered. Before his birth, his parents had promised him to Shui Sau Yuk, a country girl from Wu Sih. His duty was to this arranged marriage, set by custom to ensure his family's lineage.

He laid aside his uniform and drew Sio Ying into his arms. "You're my true love, not Sau Yuk," Pei Ching told her. Yet as he said this, he knew he could do nothing for Sio Ying.

"My destiny is bleak if I do not marry now." Sio Ying's eyes searched his face. "I have dishonored my family and myself."

He held her close, not wanting to look into her eyes. "There's no hope for us in this world, only in the next." Her body stiffened against him, yet he knew she understood the truth of his words. By the dictates of their culture, their marriage would be impossible, scandalous. "When I become wealthy, you and our child will share my success," he promised, never doubting that he would attain success.

The following week Sio Ying left the Wu house and went to the door of her mother's house; her throat tightened as she contemplated breaking her news. Head lowered she approached this formidable woman, who sat in her late husband's house, sewing the hem of a gown. Sio Ying sat on a small bamboo stool in front of her mother. "Mma, I have come to tell you something of great importance. I . . . I . . ."

"Yes. What is it? Don't sit there like a toad."

Sio Ying's mother's disposition made embers seem cool.

"I'm pregnant with Wu Pei Ching's child."

The intake of the elderly woman's breath was a dragon's hiss. Her sewing dropped, forgotten upon her lap.

"Foolish girl! What dishonor have you brought upon my head! He cannot marry you, and you cannot be his concubine. He has no money, no position. I am only the second wife here with no influence, no position of authority. I let you go to the Wu house to better yourself. Like a peasant girl you throw yourself at the young son."

It was not like that at all, Sio Ying wanted to say, but held her tongue fearing an even greater tirade.

"You will marry Yang, your childhood intended, as soon as possible. We will not tell him or his family of your condition. Understand? I will make all the arrangements with Yang's mother. I will say that the Wu house is no longer a fit place for you because of Pei Ching's father's opium habit." She paused to ponder her plan. "Yes. That will be convincing, for Yang has often said that he distrusts those with the habit. I will pressure for an immediate marriage. Yang's mother may not be so easily convinced," she said to herself while she picked at the forgotten sewing in her lap. "You're lucky my husband is dead."

Sio Ying could have argued that if her father had been alive, she would never have been sent to the Wu house, but again she remained silent. She was glad Pei Ching and she were lovers. In her heart she would never be separated from him no matter what custom dictated.

* * *

Yang married Sio Ying without knowing she was pregnant, but once he found out, he was understanding. Yang's mother, however, was not. "My grandchild will not be Yang's;" this she would never allow Sio Ying to forget.

Pei Ching, disappointed over his lost love, refused to honor the arranged marriage with Sau Yuk. When she learned of his refusal, her humiliation was great. Youth, naivete, and simplicity were her flaws as well as her strengths.

At dusk Sau Yuk trudged across the small bridge that separated the city of Wu Sih from the countryside. In the distance the hulking dome of a temple stood silhouetted against the darkening sky. Slowly and painfully her short strides carried her toward her objective. She had only recently recovered after her failed attempt at suicide when she had swallowed a golden ring. How silly she had been to believe that such a method would result in her death. That was not to be her fate. Now her only hope was to become a nun. Would she be worthy enough to be accepted?

When she finally arrived at the temple doors, the nuns

silently bade her enter. For days she lived in a small cell, ate the meager portions doled out and prayed. This place afforded her time to dwell not on her future, but on her inadequacies. Every day and night she fed her sense of abandonment by Pei Ching with self-loathing. "I'm too tall, too ugly, too plain, too uneducated." Her list grew with each passing day. It never occurred to her to harbor ill feelings toward the man who refused to honor his filial duty. After weeks of prayers to Buddha and discussions with the nuns, she still had found no comfort.

Finally her older brother came to visit her. In one of the barren rooms furnished with only a simple wooden table and chair, he confronted her. "This is no place for you, Sau Yuk. It's your responsibility to face your fate, not hide."

She gazed at her brother, noticing the stern jut of his jaw. How could he understand her humiliation? And wasn't her family also dishonored?

"We have all been enraged by Wu Pei Ching's bad behavior, but now his intransigence has passed. He has agreed to marry you after all."

Upon her return to Wu Sih, her parents said, "Now our wishes have come true, and your destiny will be fulfilled."

"I will be content," said Sau Yuk and bowed to her parents.

The following week her family gathered in front of their house to see her off to the Wu house in Wu Sih where the wedding would take place. Sau Yuk stood alone before the bridal sedan chair decorated with red embroidered cloth with tassels. Sau Yuk's tiny cousin, Zee, moved to her side and pressed a large red scarf into the bride-to-be's hand. "For your bridal headdress. We will all pray you are treated well by your new husband and his family."

After Zee walked back to the family, Sau Yuk's brother stepped forward. "We have hired one *shi nyeh* for you." Sau Yuk knew her family couldn't afford two bridal attendants as was the custom. Her family had already been generous in giving her money to rent her bridal gown and head dress. Sau Yuk nodded, unable to speak. Her lips trembled. With a last good-bye kowtow to her family, she entered the sedan and left her family. Only the groom's family would be present at the wedding; it was his family who was bringing in a daughter-in-law. Four men lifted the sedan onto their shoulders and strode forward to the Wu house. Other men walked alongside, playing flutes.

The day of the wedding her *shi nyeh* helped her dress in her rented all-red outfit of embroidered top, skirt, and her own handmade embroidered red shoes. Her headpiece was heavy with dangling beads encircling her head. Cousin Zee's red scarf draped over the headpiece and covered her face. In a small room Sau Yuk sat all day with her head and eyes lowered, her folded hands covered by different colored scarves. She was attended by her *shi nyeh*, who answered all questions directed to the bride-to-be.

"What skills do you bring to this marriage?" a Wu cousin asked.

"Sau Yuk sews beautifully," the *shi nyeh* answered.

The entire day Sau Yuk was not allowed to eat or speak; her *shi nyeh* took charge of everything.

Finally it was time for the wedding. Sau Yuk's *shi nyeh* grasped her arm and guided her into the largest room of the house. There, the Wu family and friends and Pei Ching, dressed in a short black jacket, a *ma qua*, over a navy blue gown, waited in front of the director of the wedding. This man wore a red silk tag with gold letters identifying him as a witness to the wedding.

The director bowed. "You will kneel and kowtow to heaven and earth three times." They touched their foreheads to the floor as he counted, "One kowtow, two kowtow, three kowtow. Now you will kowtow to the Wu ancestors." Again he counted out the kowtows. Sau Yuk kowtowed to her in-laws, and the couple kowtowed to the aunts and uncles, who encircled the room. Finally the director said, "You will now kowtow to each other."

The ceremony finished, the couple rose and Sau Yuk's *shi nyeh* helped her stand. "Now you have become husband and wife. I send you to the bridal room," the director said, handing the end of a long red sash, decorated with a large bow in the middle, to the groom. The *shi nyeh* put the other end of the sash into Sau Yuk's hands.

Pei Ching walked into the bridal room with Sau Yuk, together with her *shi nyeh*. The bride and the groom sat on the bed side by side. The *shi nyeh* pulled Sau Yuk's dress away so that Pei Ching could sit close. Sau Yuk sighed with relief. Apparently Pei Ching's mother had not followed the custom of bribing the *shi nyeh* to push the bride's dress under the groom as he was about to sit down to insure the bride's obedience to him. Sau Yuk trembled as Pei Ching used a small stick he'd been carrying to raise her silk scarf and uncover her face. She would liked to have looked into the eyes of her groom. If she'd been brave enough to do so, would she see acceptance, pleasure, or joy? She sensed Pei Ching's rigid body near her.

After they married, the couple fled Shanghai to escape Pei Ching's money-hungry opium-racked father; they traveled north to the Province of Shandong (Shantung). There Pei Ching worked at another arsenal under the powerful warlord, Zhang Zoulin.

For many years after their marriage, Pei Ching and Sau Yuk did not indulge in *tung fong:* theirs was a celibate marriage. Sio Ying remained the sword over the peace and happiness of the Wu Pei Ching household.

Baby Tek Ying

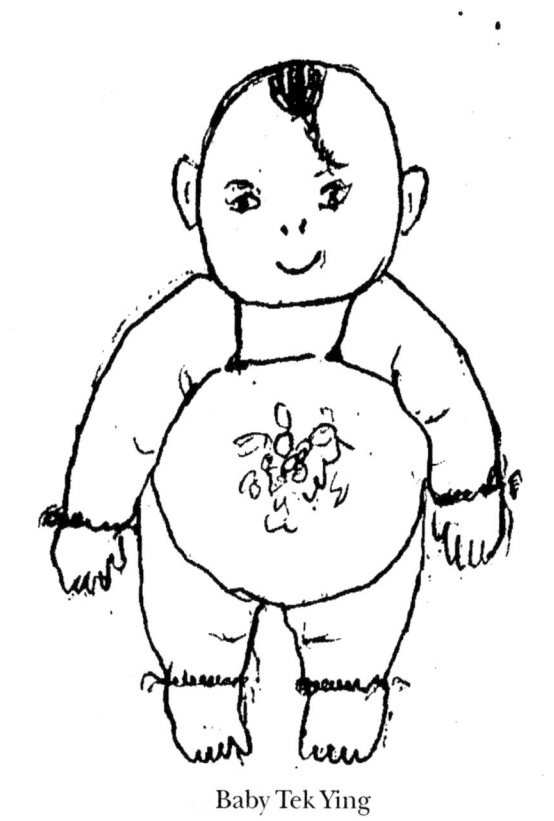

Chapter 2

1916–1927

Northern China is a land where winters freeze uncovered ears, spit turns to ice before it hits the ground, and snow piles up mountain-like on each side of shoveled pathways. In this element Sau Yuk and Pei Ching lived together while Pei Ching worked in the arsenal for the warlord, Zhang Zoulin. There, five years after my parents' marriage, I was born in 1921. My father named me "Tek Ying" after the town of my birth, Tek Chou, in Shandong Province. He called me "Tek Child."

At my birth my mother lay upon a brick bed heated by a small wood fire under the bed. Midwives came to my parents' house. As dictated by Manchurian custom, friends and relatives brought red-wrapped cone-shaped packages filled with ashes. My mother was to lay upon these, for they would absorb the afterbirth.

"A barbaric Manchurian custom," father told the midwives who hurried back and forth trying to help my mother, yet honor my father's demands. "My wife will not lie on ashes. In Shanghai women lie on paper while giving birth." "Your wife says ashes are fine," the head midwife said. "She would say that. Always deferring to others." He thrust the crumpled paper he had originally brought from his factory to use as toilet paper toward the midwife. "This paper can be used. See to it," he said, then turned his back and strode out of the house.

After my birth, a month had to pass before father could enter mother's room, "the evil blood room," since the blood associated with birth was a bad omen. I was a girl child and disappointed mother, for she believed it was her duty to have a son. Her feelings of unhappiness about having a girl child were compounded by the fact that she had learned years before that Sio Ying had had a boy child by Pei Ching. But father, unlike many Chinese men, was pleased to have a child, girl or not, and I had come into the world at the same time as his promotion in the arsenal.

"My lucky star," he said and took me from my mother's arms. My birth nurtured a deep place in his soul and our bonding bridged the tradition of the female's lesser position with the father.

"I will deliver you a boy child next time," my mother promised. Her plain face glowed, but her eyes were sad and she slumped back in her chair, bowing her head.

During the ensuing months, father continued to advance in the service of General Zhang Zoulin. As the General's power spread throughout the region, father was transferred farther north to a small town near Shenyang in Liaoning Province (formerly part of Manchuria). Mother followed, packing their few possessions and bundling me up for the journey. There we lived in seeming quiet while warlords and the Japanese army struggled against each other for power.

Two years after our arrival in Fung Tien (now Sung Yah),

mother gave birth to another girl. Father named her Fung Child in honor of the town. Both my parents had hoped for a boy, but this time mother was enamored with the baby because she was as pretty as *Yan Wa-Wa*, a foreign doll.

One day I stared at this new pink, crying addition. Tired of standing by and watching my mother feed Fung and sing lullabies to her, I tugged at mother's sleeve. "Hold me like that." I pointed to the baby.

Mother smiled, put the baby down into a woven basket and tried to pick me up and cuddle me as though I, too, were an infant. I struggled to nestle near her.

"You see. You're a big girl now, almost three. You can't be held like a baby."

I stuck my fingers in my mouth and pouted. But all was not hopeless for me. Father, when he was home, doted on me.

"Such a tiger cub you are." He tugged playfully at the single short braid hanging over my forehead. The silver anklets and bracelets he'd bought for me jangled.

"Why do you spend money on such ornaments?" mother asked. "She doesn't understand their meaning."

"Money is to be spent." Father flicked his fingers against one of the charms. "It shows my affection. Do you deny me this?"

"No, no, Tek Child's father." Mother's voice trembled. "I delight in your delight of her."

It was a cold winter day, and mother was keeping herself busy indoors, layering bits of cloth swatches with flour paste to make soles for our shoes. Father studied her for a long time, then stormed about the room, gathering up the pile of saved bits and pieces of cloth and tossing them into the fire that warmed the brick bed.

"Enough! You drive me crazy with your scrimping. Don't I give you enough money for clothes? You shame me. I have a good position, make good money. There's no need for this . . . this peasant work."

Mother cringed. "But Tek Child's father, it's wasteful. The shoes will be nice."

"You make people think I am poor."

Tears welled up in her eyes. "I don't mean to displease you."

Father sighed and looked away. He did not smile again until he looked at me just as the rich oily egg yolk I was attempting to eat dribbled down my chin. He laughed. "Tiger cub has a yellow beard. See the glint in her eyes. She will not easily be tamed."

In-between my father's infrequent appearances in my early life, my days were spent with my mother. In the small town of Fung Tien, I often accompanied her when she went to the Buddhist temple, trotting beside her, grasping her hand. At the time I didn't notice her humble square cut gray jacket and long black skirt, nor her hair pulled back in a chignon, which accentuated her plain features.

She always carried a bag of incense and bought a bag of red Chinese dates from the street vendor. Behind us beggars scurried through the crowd. When one pushed too close, she reached into her date bag and dropped a few into his outstretched hand. Immediately, he darted after other temple-goers. When his pockets bulged with dates, he hurried to the nearest date vendor. The vendor weighed the beggar's dates, paid him in coins and later resold them. His great magical mound of dates never diminished.

Life seemed magical to me in many ways. On the 23rd day of the 12th month, according to the Chinese calendar the lunar month, we, like most Chinese, recognized the custom of the Kitchen god. I looked on while mother placed a picture of the Kitchen God in a small pagoda-like holder over the built-in stove.

I helped her light candles and incense. Then she placed dishes of food and candles in front of the god's picture and forbade me to take any of them; they were for the god, not little children. "Sticky candy is put on the god's mouth to sweeten it," she explained to me as she pushed the candy onto the picture. She pulled me down next to her as she knelt and began to pray to the god. "Our family has been good this past year," she told the Kitchen God. "Tek Child's father had another promotion. I have cooked many good meals and have brought my daughter to the temple many times."

She continued to say only sweet things about us. If the Kitchen God reported bad things to the Heavenly God, punishment and bad fortune would come to my family. But hearing sweet things about my family, the Heavenly God would bless us with good fortune. After mother had conducted the ceremony, she burned the Kitchen God's picture to see him off to heaven.

On the 30th day of the 12th lunar month, mother and I welcomed the Kitchen God back from heaven. We bought a new picture to place over the stove. Again she performed a similar ceremony as before, thanking the Kitchen God for delivering her message about our wonderful family to the heavenly God. But this time she didn't put sticky candy on the god's mouth.

When mother conducted this custom, I believed all would always be well with my family and me. However, with the passing years the Kitchen God was not always kind to my family.

Father was seldom with us, even on special days, and was away from home much of the time. As a child I never questioned his absence and thought all families were like ours. When he was home, my parents argued about nothing and everything.

"What will people say about our having two girls?" mother pestered him.

"I don't care what people think!" father said.

"Should I keep Tek Child in the house? Or maybe I

should only take one of the girls out at a time. I do wish she'd been a boy."

"If it bothers you so much, why don't you dress Tek Child like a boy. She's too young to know the difference."

The following day mother set to work to transform me into looking like a boy. She dressed me in a boy's long gown, vest, and a fur hat with earmuffs. While tears ran down my face, she shaved my head, leaving only a rim of bangs that went all around my head.

While I was treated like a boy, my baby sister was cuddled and dressed up in lovely girl costumes. Everyone thought she was beautiful. Mrs. Chang, our childless neighbor, was enamored with Fung Child. One day she came over to our house and after endless cooing over my sister, she said, "I'm going to the opera tonight. Please, let me take Fung Child with me so I may show her off."

I had heard about the loud opera music and seen pictures of the actors dressed up with painted faces. How exciting it would be to go to the opera. I should be taken instead of my baby sister.

I watched as my mother dressed my sister in a lavender cape embroidered and trimmed in silver with a bonnet to match. When Mrs. Chang and her maidservant left our house carrying my seven-month-old sister, I pouted in the back room, tugging at my long boyish coat. Mrs. Chang was not interested in showing off a girl dressed as a boy.

"Stupid," I said to no one. "She won't like it."

The following day my little sister fell ill with a high fever. Father, as usual, was away, and mother fretted and called in every doctor and every woman in Fung Tien with any medical knowledge to help save Fung Child. The house felt small as it filled with friends and neighbors. Candles flickered late into the night, and my baby sister was swaddled with cool cloths. In the morning my beautiful baby sister was dead. Had she liked the opera?

Mother knelt by the brick bed where she'd lain Fung Child's body and sobbed in pain. Her small half-bound feet pounded up and down on the hard floor. I stood next to her crying, too. I turned and watched the tears stream down mother's face and tried to match her sob for sob. It was very tiring and I wondered how long I would have to stay next to her. My legs hurt, but I didn't dare make a fuss. Mother was in pain. What could I do for her?

Eventually, a manservant tapped me on the shoulder, took me by the hand and led me into the yard. There he and I stayed for what seemed like hours kicking stones and walking around in circles. The icy wind blew against us, but I was numb to its sting. Where had my baby sister gone and when would my mother's sad face be happy again?

Unfortunately for mother, father and me, the impact of my baby sister's death stayed with my mother forever. From that time on, dolls were unacceptable for me, for they reminded my mother of Fung Child.

Beauty died and I lived. What did that say about me? Had my jealousy of my baby sister caused the tragedy? I pushed such thoughts aside. Father returned in time for Fung Child's burial, but left immediately afterwards for another assignment.

Mother tried to put aside her grieving and took me to a holiday fair held in the town's garden, called *Shiu Hoa Yuen*. Throngs of parents and children moved eagerly from one entertainment to another. Mother and I walked through the park surrounding a small pond with pink and white water lilies. In awe we watched the elegant ladies from Fung Tien strolling near us. Their elaborate headdresses in the shape of an inverted canoe were typical of the Manchurian style. Their shoes with lifts like sailboat keels in the middle of the soles produced a short rolling gait. Unlike other Chinese women of that period, the Manchus and the Mongols did not practice footbinding. My mother, typical of her era, had deformed shaped feet with broken arches and curled toes. The result of the footbinding, beside the pain, was that mother could only put weight on the back edge of her heel. These Manchurian women were not affected by this cruel tradition and walked erect, proud of their stylish garb, a sharp contrast to my mother's plain clothes and my boyish dress.

After a while the spectacle of the passing fashion parade bored me. I heard music and ran forward, pulling mother by the hand to view a group of acrobats six to ten years old. They balanced full water glasses on their heads and turned somersaults.

Drummer Girl

Nearby a *Daikoo* or "Sing Song" girl sang and smartly kept time on a small drum supported by a tripod. "Rat-a-tat, rat-a-tat." Her songs were stories most everyone knew. Seated in front of her in chairs men smoked water pipes, watched the performance and chatted with one another. Women sat next to them, cracking watermelon seeds with their teeth and spitting the shells onto the ground.

I would have watched and listened to the performances until the end, but mother had tired easily from standing and walking the long distance. She pulled me away from the magical world and took me home.

The following day, I, too, was a Daikoo girl and an acrobat. I made a toy drum from a pot and used chop sticks for drumsticks. As I beat out a rhythm I sang loudly. Then I lay down and balanced a glass of water on my forehead. When I tried to stand up, mother ran to stop me. Too late. The glass shattered and water ran down my back.

While mother picked up the mess she scolded, "Those children in the acrobat group are not so lucky. They'd be beaten for making a mess. It's not so easy if you are sold and forced to learn to perform such acts."

I understood her words, but not their implication. I only knew my imaginative play had been thwarted.

Father had been away from the house for a week and mother became grumpier than usual. When she sent me to get him, I was thrilled. She ordered the rickshaw man to take me to the painted house with colored lanterns hanging in the front. Off I went to bring him back from a *Yao-Chih*.

When I arrived, father greeted me. "Tek? Tek Child! You . . . here? Ah . . . " He clasped my hand then moved away from me, as ladies with beautiful painted faces flocked around to greet and play with me. I touched their long, blue uniform-like cotton dresses, amazed at the soft texture. Their fingers sparkled with rings; their arms jangled with bracelets; their high collars were adorned with necklaces. With an open mouth and wide eyes, I watched as they held hands and danced in a circle about me as though

I were a toy. I had never been the center of attention by so many interested and well-meaning ladies. One of the ladies remained standing next to my father. Through the throng of ladies encircling me, I caught a glimpse of my father's wide smile as he looked at the lady. She whispered in his ear and then came forward and pressed candies into my hands. Others filled my arms with toys. I had never had so many toys. Beaming with joy, I was shown out of the *Yao Chih,* ensconced back in the rickshaw surrounded by presents stacked on the seat, on the foot rest, and even on the folded back cover of the rickshaw, and returned home. The rickshaw man helped me down. Together he and I gathered up my booty. I rushed into the house eager to show mother my new treasures.

When mother saw me come in alone, her face clouded. Proudly I extended my arms loaded with the presents toward her. She slapped my candies onto the floor. They spun like dice across the wood floor. I cried out, "What . . . ? They were given to me by father's lovely lady friends."

"I sent you to get your father, not to come home with bribes!"

Later that night when father came home, I lay in bed and heard him shout at mother. "What crazy idea made you send a child to a *"Yao-Chih?"*

"Look at you," mother yelled back. "Those women refaced your gown. What am I to think?"

"It's none of your business!"

"Where did you get your new watch chain? Those initials aren't yours. Are they from your girl at the *Yao-Chih?"*

"I like it! Why don't you think of spending money to make me happy?"

Father continued to berate mother for her interference and frugality, and mother sputtered her anger over his frequent visits to the *Yao-Chih*. I pulled the quilt over my head and eventually fell asleep to the strum of their angry words.

The following morning father strode off to work before I even had a chance to say "good morning" to him. I ran outside only to see his black gown disappear into the morning fog. Restless for something to do, I scratched faces in the dirt with a stick and listened to our manservant chatting with a friend. "My master works for the powerful General Zhang Zoulin."

His friend spat at the base of a nearby brick wall. "He was a peasant, an enlisted man."

"Once a peasant, now military governor of Fengtian. A great feat," our manservant countered.

The friend looked around, lowered his voice and said, "The army is a dragon eating our families."

Our servant stood straighter. "Not Zhang Zoulin's!"

"He'll lose to the 'dog meat general,'" the friend said.

Our servant laughed. "No, no one can compete with Zhang Zhongchang's love for dog meat. But Shandong Province's warlord wouldn't dare attack our General here in Manchuria."

The other man shook his head. "Pray to Buddha you are right. Dog meat General's men are butchers. They left a trail of split skulls hanging from telegraph poles when he conquered southern Shandong. I saw them. They looked like rows of open watermelons on spikes."

I covered my ears and backed into our doorway. Is that what warlords do? I closed my eyes and visualized the rows of poles. I stifled my cry, sucked in my breath, and although half-afraid, continued to listen. What other terrible things would I hear?

"Zhongchang must be great," our servant's friend said. "He has forty concubines of different nationalities each with her own washbowl marked with the flag of her nation."

Our servant chuckled and muttered something in

return as the two men walked out into the street. I was left with a vision of forty women lined up in front of washbowls. The next time mother sent me to pick up my father I was less exuberant, since I was to go to the arsenal. I thought of "the dog meat general" and prayed my father, who was now a major general under General Zhang Zoulin, would never have to meet him.

To please me and perhaps to further his standing with my father, our rickshaw man had decorated the rickshaw with pink-colored flowers—phoenix flowers—on the square glass side lanterns of the rickshaw. The flowers looked like lovely birds in a cage. I sat back, pretending to be a queen and enjoyed seeing the sun sag behind the purple-tinged hills that laced the far side of the valley of Liaoning Province. But when we entered the gates to the arsenal, I cringed at the rows of stern-faced soldiers lining the road. Suddenly they raised their guns in the air and gave out great shouts. I burst into tears.

When I ran into father's office sobbing, he took me in his arms, patted me, and laughed. "Silly child. They are honoring you with a salute. I'm their commander; you are my child. It's a show of respect."

Back home father tried to soothe my worries about armies and warlords by telling mother and me about General Zhang Zoulin's huge underground storage room full of his treasures. "I believe he wanted to reinforce the belief that it was he who was the 'The little king of the north,' not Zhang Zhongchang," he said.

I shuddered at the "dog meat general's" name.

"Are you cold, Tek Child?" he asked.

I shook my head and cuddled closer to him as I sat on his lap. Mother sat across from us listening with obvious interest to father's description of the room of treasures.

"I walked into that treasure room and sank into a thick carpet of wolf's fur. You know how soft an animal's fur is under its chin and around its neck; well, that's how soft the fur was. There was jade carved like plant leaves, with rubies representing seeds in the plants' centers; a jade carved watermelon with rubies and black jade carved to look like the inside of the melon; bricks of gold stacked around the room." Father gestured with his arm, showing the height of the gold mound. "Rosewood furniture inlaid with precious stones was pushed up against the walls like cords of wood."

Later that night as I lay in bed, gleaming jade and rubies simmered in my thoughts, images so real, so dazzling that I remember them today. Where those treasures came from was never discussed. The booty of the warlords taken from the areas they conquered was of no concern to me then. Had I known that the Wu family would know both sides of prosperity's door, I might have reacted differently to the tale of the treasure trove.

* * *

Despite my father's position we led a simple life, although daily activities were often thwarted by overzealous police. Once, I accompanied mother to visit friends. I romped in the yard with other children while mother played Mah-jongg for fun and small stakes, even though it was forbidden. Suddenly people shouted, "The police are coming to arrest someone!" The crowd scattered. My playmates ran for cover. I scampered toward the back of the yard, fearing the worst for my poor mother.

There I scrambled into a discarded oven and curled up into a tiny ball. The din of confusion and shouting continued. I pictured my mother being hauled off to jail, and I cried in my small hiding place. Soon the shouting died, but I didn't move. Finally I heard my father call my name. My muffled answering cry echoed in the oven. His strong hands rescued my ash-covered quacking body.

"Don't fret, now. I've taken care of everything. Your mother sent for me as soon as the police arrived. I'm sending my aide to the police with a protest. I'll have an apology from them within the day." I believed Father could manage any situation.

Soon after this incident, father was sent to Japan for four months as an envoy of General Zhang Zoulin. He traveled to different cities—Osaka, Kobe, Tokyo, and Kyoto, where he stayed the longest. Mother got one letter from the Miyako Hotel in Kyoto. It seemed as if he were gone for years, but months later he returned and once again mother and I sat and listened to his stories. I sat on his lap, absorbed in the pictures he had brought home. His voice vibrated with excitement. Mother stared at the floor. Why wasn't mother as happy as I to hear of his tales about Japanese geisha houses?

"Because of my high position, I was entertained royally," father said. "Once an important official and his wife took me to a Japanese *Ofuro*. That's a large indoor bathing place. While I luxuriated in the water, I was shocked to see the official's wife enter the room, remove her kimono, wash the lower portion of her body with water from a bucket of water standing along side the pool, and step into the bath to join us.

"I was so startled by her boldness, that without thinking, I scrambled out of the bath, threw on my clothes, and hurried back to my hotel. Only later did my interpreter tell me that the wife's behavior was perfectly acceptable in the Japanese culture." He laughed at his retelling the incident.

Mother leaned forward, apparently intrigued despite herself by the strangeness of this custom.

Father launched into another story. "I found one of the ladies in a geisha house so enticing that I moved from my hotel into that house," he began.

Mother's body stiffened.

"One morning in the general room I was surprised to

see everyone elaborately dressed. When I saw my special geisha girl parade in wearing a white brocade wedding kimono, I knew I'd used the Japanese word for YES at the wrong time." He paused and smiled at me. "I must admit my reliance on my dictionary got me into big trouble. I was so sure I had the word right."

He squeezed my hand and turned to mother. "Tek Child's mother, you'll be pleased that I didn't bring home a Japanese concubine like some of my friends. Instead, I retreated back to my hotel, a little wiser in the use of my Japanese-Chinese dictionary."

Mother didn't answer; she just rose and left the room.

These tales furthered my idolization of my father, but for mother they must have been agony. I accepted my parents' love toward me with little understanding of their stormy relationship, and their love nourished me, despite their personal problems. Even the death of my grandfather on my father's side left me with memories that nurtured my idolization of my father.

After we heard of grandfather's death, father traveled alone all the way to Wu Sih from northern China—a hard journey that took many days on a train and a boat. Upon his arrival in Wu Sih, father discovered that his father had piled up debts brought on by his need to supply his opium habit. Unwilling to let my grandfather's name be disgraced, father posted a sign outside grandfather's house after the funeral. "Should my father owe anyone money, please come forward. I will pay the amount without asking questions."

My father showed his love and respect for his father by insuring that he would be respected as someone who honored his debts. In China being a filial son was honorable. The ancient tales I had heard about the twenty-four filial sons made me think my father must be the twenty-fifth filial son.

One of these stories tells of a mother who fell ill during the winter and asked for nothing but a piece of fresh fish. But the lake was frozen so deeply that catching a fish was impossible. Her son was so determined that his mother should have her fish that he stretched out on the frozen lake and slept there, hoping to melt the ice. This act touched the heavenly god, and soon the frozen spot where the son slept melted and formed a hole. Out of the hole jumped a fish, which the grateful son happily took home to his mother.

Another filial son story took place in the hot summer. Mosquitoes buzzed ceiling to floor, and sleeping restfully was impossible. A son seeing his mother's discomfort told her to go into another room; as soon as she left, he climbed into her bed inside the curtains and lay there allowing the mosquitoes to bite him until they were sated with his blood. Only then did the filial son lead his mother to her bed, knowing she would pass the night peacefully.

Despite Father's sorrow over his last visit to Wu Sih for his father's funeral, we all enjoyed the next summer in my grandmother's countryside home.

"Come, Tek Child," grandmother would say, "we will dance in the fields before the warm summer sun falls." She took my hand and led me into the green vegetable fields while she gathered special herbs. To her this was dancing with nature, and I always felt that's exactly what she and I did in the fields.

When we came back to the house, she plopped down in a chair on the porch and shared the sweet center of a watermelon with me. "I wonder what you will be when you grow up? You must go to school. Your father will see to that. But there are more things to learn other than what's in a book."

Suddenly several women from the village hurried down the path to grandmother's house.

"Medicine Woman," one woman called out, holding a young boy about my age in her arms. "My son is ill with heat blisters. Can you help?"

Although grandmother wasn't a doctor, she was well-known for her success in helping the sick or injured. Country children often suffered an outbreak of blisters during the scorching hot summers. I watched from the doorway as grandmother put the suffering child onto a table. Sweat poured down my face, but grandmother's face was unperturbed. She seemed untouched by the heat and the wails of the child. The boy's blister had become infected and swelled up to egg size. She disinfected a small knife by holding it over a candle flame, and opened and drained the blister. I held my breath, hunched my shoulders in awe, and squinted. I relaxed again only when the boy stopped screaming and his sobs came in gulps. Grandmother cleaned the wound and dressed it with Chinese herbs that she kept in small straw boxes.

Without receiving payment, only the thanks of the mother, grandmother came back out on the porch and continued to eat watermelon as though nothing of import had occurred.

That same summer the daughter of Lok Hsiao-ming, the man father hired to manage grandmother's farm, dislocated her shoulder when she fell into a ditch. Her mother scooped her up in her arms and hurried to grandmother, who immediately readjusted the little girl's shoulder and soothed her pain.

One morning I awoke and overheard grandmother chatting with my mother. "I had to use the ma-tung (chamber pot) and groped under my bed for my slippers. What do you think I got hold of? A mouse."

"I didn't hear you cry out," mother said.

"Why should I cry out? It was only a mouse. I picked up a small knife from my bedside table, cut the mouse up and tossed it into the ma-tung."

I saw mother turn away with a queasy look on her face. I thought grandmother was very brave, but I didn't want to see the cut-up mouse. I had an unusual fear of any kind of animal or bird and I would have screamed and screamed if I had touched a mouse as my grandmother had.

Most of the time I played within sight of the adults, but their conversations were usually dull annoying throbs intruding on my world of make-believe. One day when I heard sharp words between my mother, grandmother and my father, I stopped playing to listen. Mother saw me staring and sent me outside to play, but I couldn't help overhearing the raging voices from within the thin-walled house.

"He's your son," my mother said. "If you wish to adopt Sio Ying's and your child, I'll agree."

"For now Yang has accepted my son." Father's voice was low and steady. "But the mother-in-law dotes only on Sio Ying's and Yang's daughter and ignores Gun Yuen. I want to do better for him."

"Not possible, not possible," grandmother's voice echoed out the window. "The scandal would be terrible. He's Yang's son now. It's unthinkable! Forget Sio Ying's child. You have your own family now. Past deeds must be forgotten, buried!"

Further words spilled forth, but since I didn't understand their implication, I went to play with Lok Hsiao-ming's daughter.

Soon after this row, father departed for Fung Tien while mother and I remained for a longer visit. But before father left, he gifted grandmother with more land, which seemed to be the only possession she desired. Lok Hsiao-ming took on the added responsibilities of managing the larger piece of property. Father's land purchases were well-timed, for Wu Sih was becoming a thriving mill town with several large landowners taking charge of the local government. Father's purchases seemed to assure the family's prosperity.

Chapter 3

1928

As a child, little did I understand how my father's working for Zhang Zoulin affected my mother's and my life. Like small crickets we were captured by history and flung up and down in a cage not of our making. My father, like most Chinese men, made the rules by which we played. He in turn was caught in the web of history and torn by loyalties.

Father came under increasing pressure as the warlords fought each other as well as the Japanese. Although losing several areas to other warlords, General Zhang still governed Manchuria. As one of Zhang Zoulin's Major Generals, father must have known the tide was turning. Before the Japanese sent troops to Shandong Province in 1927, father decided my mother and I would be safer in Shanghai. His military duties demanded that he stay in Fung Tien, but in 1926 he sent mother and me to Shanghai and traveled part of the way with us to make sure we wouldn't have any problems.

Like bookends, I was protected by my father and mother

on either side, each holding my hand as we pushed our way through the crowded train station to buy our tickets. The dark station smelled of anxious, sweating humans. Impatient men and women elbowed each other for a place in the ticket window line.

"Wait here," father commanded. He strode off, not for the ticket line but in search of the stationmaster. I clung to mother as we stood apart from the shoving crowd, our luggage piled around us. When he pushed his way back through the crowd, our tickets in hand, I almost shouted with relief. Moments later men loaded our luggage aboard the comfortable first class car with the padded soft seats. Father had made sure we wouldn't have to ride in the cars that had bare hard wooden seats.

Father accompanied us as far as Tientsien (now Tianjin). The following day when father helped mother and me climb onto the train for the rest of the trip to Shanghai, I cried, clung to his leg and refused to let him go.

"Here's some candy, and dried fruit, Tek Child," he said, leaning down to me.

I shook my head, refusing to give in to his bribe.

"Here is the best part." He showed me a toy scale he'd hidden behind his back. "You must weigh the candy and fruit. Can you be a shopkeeper and tell your mother how much it costs?"

I released my death grip on his leg and took the scale. Before long I was in the train seated next to mother. While our train headed south toward Shanghai and a new beginning, father returned to Fung Tien in the north.

Upon our arrival in Shanghai, mother left our luggage in the hotel room father had reserved for us, and she and I made our way to "Chu Hun Li," the home of my Uncle Chu's two widowed wives. We knew they would expect us to stay with them, but it would have been presumptuous to arrive with our luggage. It was important that we observe the niceties of an invitation first.

Father would have been angry if he'd known where we went before going to the Chus. He and mother were at odds on how money should be spent. Father wanted the best he could buy, while mother wanted only the cheapest she could find. Here in Shanghai Mother's timidity gave in to her desire for bargains.

She led me down a crowded noisy street of secondhand clothing shops. Vendors shouted; buyers argued. We passed a market loud with singing and squawking caged birds and fowls. I stopped momentarily in front of a chemist's shop to gawk at the bottles of dried lizards and pickled salamanders. Mother gave my hand a sharp tug, and we continued pushing our way through this new world. The loud "click click" of the abacus as merchants counted their sales joined into the rhythms of the "clip clop" of ponies' hooves as they pulled loaded carts.

In front of each store stood a vendor singing out the virtues of the garment he had plucked from the cloth-wrapped bundle beside him on the sidewalk. Holding the shirt or gown high above his head, he called out its remarkable qualities, "Very strong and warm in cold weather—only five yuan." If the vendor spotted an interested gleam in an eye, he moved in to negotiate a sale. Then both seller's and potential buyer's voices escalated as they bargained back and forth. If the crowd started to dwindle, the vendor folded the garment, laid it aside, and searched his bundle for another perhaps more appealing "remarkable" bargain.

While mother stood absorbed with the shouting sales pitch of a vendor, I wandered into the shop behind him. In front of me on a rack was a beautiful sea-blue silk sash. I turned and ran to drag mother into the store.

"Look! How beautiful. I want it!" I cried out.

"Not now. We've just arrived. Perhaps later." She tried to pull me away.

"I want it! Father would like me to have it."

She shook her head. "It doesn't go with your long gown."
"I don't care." I stamped my foot. "I want it!"

A few minutes later, having won, I tied the new sash around my waist with a large bow, and I strode next to mother, now more confident. We turned a corner and watched bicycles jostle against carts loaded with fruits and vegetables and pulled by men or women or children. Thin sweating coolies, naked to the waist, pushed wheelbarrows. Others balanced long shoulder-poles swaying with baskets full of trussed squawking geese and chickens. On yet another street these same scenes were juxtaposed against passing black automobiles. The tooting of car horns mingled with the chatter of people and the ringing of bicycle bells.

In the distance massive concrete western-style buildings with spires, clock towers, and domes rose upward. My neck muscles began to knot from constantly looking skyward. The facades of Chinese figurations on the front of the three and four story buildings intrigued me. Overhangs part way up the buildings looked like eyebrows. A jumble of spires, turrets, or domes topped the buildings, and I stared openmouthed. Like pebbles in a river bumping along through the clotted stream of humanity, mother and I moved forward. I held tight to her hand, but she, too, seemed to be overcome by the sheer size of the buildings, the throngs of people, the sounds of a city writhing with life, and a thousand scents.

Finally, mother's half-bound feet could take no more walking, and we climbed into a rickshaw. Mother asked the man to take us to Won Chou Road in the British section of Shanghai, a crowded area where narrow dirty lanes separated the houses. After dismounting from the rickshaw, we stood for a moment staring at Auntie Chu's house—a U-shaped compound that faced the busy street. The U-type two-story rental apartment complex was called a *Li*. The apartments faced onto a middle lane that ran up to one large private house with an east and west wing. These wings were separated by a patio and a large hall that was used for special occasions. The servants lived behind the house. In the rear along the width of the main house lay a large area where the family's rickshaws were kept and where the servants carried out their duties.

Mother and I held hands as we took hesitant steps toward the main house and this new world. A house servant answered our knock and led us into the room where my aunties awaited us.

Tek Ying Dressed As A Boy

They grasped our hands warmly, but giggled and gave me sidelong glances. What was wrong? I wondered.

"*Little Shen Tung,*" I heard them whisper. Why did they call me a little Barbarian?

"You must excuse her northern Mandarin dialect," mother said.

"Don't worry," Uncle Chu's first wife, Auntie Chu, said. "This will change as she lives in Shanghai. But why is she wearing the dress of a boy?"

"And that strange sash," Second Auntie Chu said.

"She just had to have it," mother said, "as a memory of

her coming to Shanghai." Mother motioned me forward. "This is Auntie Chu, Uncle Chu's first wife. And this is Uncle Chu's second wife. You will call her Second Auntie Chu."

Since Uncle Chu's death, Auntie Chu's position as the respectable first wife meant that she would probably never re-marry. However, the younger and lovely Second Auntie Chu, whom Uncle Chu had taken from a *Yao-Chih*, could remarry. As second wife she held little, if any, position of power in the house.

After I greeted my aunties with low bows, mother and I were shown to our quarters in the west wing. My aunties lived in the east wing with their son. Our servants brought our luggage from the hotel, and mother and I settled in to live with the Chus, just as my parents had expected.

From a window in my room, I could see distant rooftops covered with grayish-black clay tiles. Below me lay the brick-paved patio. Twining green and purple morning glories rose column-like from large pots placed against the patio wall. I came to have a part in their lushness. My aunties kept a small chamber pot (ma-tung) for me only to use. When I filled it half way up, Auntie Chu added water and fertilized the morning glories. I was proud that I had something to do with the flowers' profuse blooming.

Even though Shanghai was the biggest and most modern city in China, at the time I lived there, almost three-fourths of the families had no bathroom facilities. Instead, for taking care of human waste, each family used at least two ma-tungs (horse buckets). The buckets had a lid and a handle and were kept in a small room or under the stairs. Poor families who had only one room kept their ma-tungs behind their beds. The ma-tungs the adults used served an even more important purpose. Their night-soil served to enrich the land so China could produce enough crops to sustain its population. The waste collection of night soil was such a lucrative business that the underworld became involved in the operation. My Aunties often talked about Cassia Ma, the Nightsoil Queen, who dominated the waste collection business in Shanghai.

Late in the night the maidservants replaced the used ma-tungs with clean ones and carried the used ones out to the street. Around three or four o'clock in the morning a waste collector arrived hauling a large container. He moved from house to house, street by street transferring the waste from the ma-tungs to the container.

Later, at five or six in the morning, sleepy servants from each house carried out the ma-tung cleaning tools—a bamboo brush, a bunch of small rough shells, and water. They poured water and shells into the empty ma-tungs and vigorously swished the shells around with the bamboo brush until the ma-tungs were clean. Although cleaning the ma-tungs was an unpleasant task, doing so gave the maids time to gather in the street and chat with neighboring servants, and to laugh and gossip about the affairs of their respective families' houses. The early morning chatter of the maids and the "swishing" stirred me out of sleep.

"Ah-Cha, (sister) I have to tell you. Last night our Lau Ya (big master) didn't come home and his second Tai-Tai (wife) cried and complained to the first Tai-Tai. Then the first Tai-Tai said, 'It seems you've lost your charm. Perhaps we will have a third Tai-Tai in our house.' Ah-yah! Ah-yah! The second Tai-Tai cried and cursed."

Not to be outdone another maid broke in, "Well, in our house the second Tai-Tai disappeared. She'd had an affair with our Lau Ya's private accountant. Our Lau Ya caught them in bed, kicked her out and fired the accountant."

Almost reluctantly they put away their tools and strolled indoors to continue their daily chores. Since I had few toys and no other children to play with, I concocted my own game of ma-tung cleaning with an empty cigarette can, a discarded incense stick, and small clam shells retrieved from the kitchen. That's how I imitated the maids' morning ritual.

Mimicking others became a source of play for me. Since my aunties had called me the little barbarian, mother began to dress me like a girl. However, the clothes she chose for me made me look like a little old woman, and I longed to be fashionable. With fascination I watched the ladies' daily hairdressing rituals. Early every morning the hairdresser hurried down the street, stopping at each of her client's houses to make the lady presentable for the day. Out would come each lady's hairdressing box, containing a mirror which slid into an upright position, small bottles of fragrant oil, a round piece of embroidered silk, several double-sided combs, and strands of bound hair for more elaborate hair styles. Sometimes the hairdresser combed, cleaned, and styled the lady's hair in her own bedroom, while at other times the lady set her box up on a table surrounded by neighbors or friends. Laughing and chatting, they waited while the hairdresser fine-combed the lady's waist-length hair, dabbed sweet-smelling oil on the embroidered silk piece and slicked down each stray hair. As a final touch she twirled the lady's hair into a chignon, secured it with hairpins, and decorated it with gold, silver, pearl, or jade stickpins. Sometimes the hairdresser intertwined silk threads with the chignon hair strands. Mother usually chose lavender thread; I liked the way she looked and smelled at the end of these sessions.

After everyone left the room, I sat in front of mother's hairdressing box and took out one of the long silken strands of hair. Opening the drawer of the table, I secured the end of the hairpiece in the drawer and braided and twirled the hair, pretending to be a hairdresser. Time flew by while I pretended to be a busy grown-up woman.

However, there was a limit to my imaginative play, and on rainy days I was particularly bored. "Mother, will you play a game with me?"

"Not now. Play by yourself."

"I had friends in the north to play with. There are no children here. Father would play with me if he were here."

"But he is not here and you must act like a little lady in the Chu's house."

I stood alone in the front hall for a few minutes, then grabbed my white lamb skin gown from the dowel by the front door, pulled it inside out so that the woolly lining was on the outside, and ran to stand in the rain. I'd show her! The rain penetrated, soaking the lining. This would make mother as miserable as I was.

After a few moments the front door banged open. Mother scurried toward me and dragged me inside. "What are you thinking of?" She slapped my bottom. "You've ruined a good gown. What if you got sick?"

Stubbornly, I stood like a tree, with water puddling around my feet. She yanked off my wet garment, stared at me for a moment, then fled into the kitchen, crying. As I later reflected, I wondered if my naughtiness was too much for her, or was her life's fountain so full of unhappiness that it took little to make it overflow?

My idle days at the Chus were interrupted when news came that my "Medicine Woman grandmother" in Wu Sih had died. Mother and I traveled the short distance from Shanghai to grandmother's, but father's journey from the north once again took him many days.

I felt a large weight upon me, but didn't fully understand the import of her death. I only knew my grandmother would no longer sit and eat watermelon with me outside in the heat of a summer day.

At my father's midnight arrival the family gathered to join in weeping in the room where my grandmother's body lay. Father knelt by her coffin and wept openly. Auntie Yuk Ching, Father's youngest sister, looked on wide-eyed at "Big Brother's" unexpected crying. She could cry only without tears, for she had wept all her tears earlier.

During this winter stay in Wu Sih as I sat in the kitchen eating my morning bowl of congee (rice gruel), Auntie Yuk Ching told me about the jagged scar on my father's upper arm. I had often run my tiny fingers along it and asked him where it came from, but he always told me to run along and play.

"Once, long ago, your grandmother became seriously ill." Auntie Yuk Ching sat down at the wood table with a cup of hot jasmine tea. Only when she saw I had stopped eating and was listening did she continue. "The family prayed for her to the heavenly God and burned incense to help her get well, but there seemed to be no hope. One night while grandmother was sleeping and your father sat alone with her, he took hold of the inside of his arm with his teeth, like this." She mimicked the act. I cringed. "He cut out his raised flesh with scissors." She picked up a nearby scissors and snipped at the air. I dropped my chopsticks into my rice bowl. "After patting incense ashes on the cut to stop the bleeding, he dropped the piece of flesh into a pot of boiling water and cooked it to make broth. He fed this broth to her, letting no one except God know what he had done; if he told anyone, your grandmother wouldn't be cured." She reached across the table and patted my arm. "But I knew. Your grandmother recovered so you would be able to know her and she could love you."

My father was surely the twenty-fifth filial son.

During father's stay with us at the Auntie Chus, Sio Ying, father's first love, arrived. I stood open-mouthed staring at her elegant clothes. She wore a short waistline jacket with a curved hem and large open lined sleeves with lace at the edges. Her small upper lip lifted in a simpering smile, showing her even pearl white teeth.

"I have come to see Pei Ching," she announced. She minced her way into the Chus' house, her head swaying as though it were attached to her body by a spring. She, too, had half-bound feet like my mother, yet she seemed to glide seductively.

Mother bowed, scuffing her feet on the floor. Compared to Sio Ying she was dowdy in her square-cut jacket and long black pants. Only mother's hair was decorated, since she was in the first year of mourning for grandmother and the second year of mourning for grandfather. To show her respect for her husband's parents, she had to wear white yarn wrapped into the middle of her chignon for the first year of mourning and yellow yarn for the second year. In the third year she would wear blue.

Mother's cheeks turned red as she spoke to Sio Ying. "He's in bed. Come back later when he's up."

No sooner had the words tumbled from mother's mouth than Sio Ying sidled off toward father's room. Before she reached his room, he stepped out on the landing, dressed in silk Chinese pajamas and robe.

"Sio Ying," he said, taking her hands in his. His face broke into a broad smile. Without looking back at mother, Sio Ying entered father's bedroom after him and closed the door behind her. Her perfume, a sweet cloying odor, wafted down the hall. Mother tiptoed up to the door and peeked through the keyhole. When she turned away, tears were streaming down her cheeks.

Shortly after Sio Ying left the house, my father and mother shouted at each other in his bedroom. I heard Sio Ying's name many times. Out in the hall I put my hands together and prayed. "Please, don't let them fight this time too."

"You gave her money. I saw you." mother said.

"Yes, I did. It's none of your business," father shouted.

"You two treat me like I don't exist."

"Enough! I do what I must. I promised to take care of Sio Ying and my son. If I did not honor my obligations, then you would have cause to weep."

Their bickering continued. I ran to my room and tried to forget their harsh words.

While father was staying with us, mother became

pregnant again. Throughout this pregnancy she often visited the temple of the *Lu Han* Buddha. There along with other pregnant women she prayed to the 500 small red-hatted Buddhas to help her bear a son. Mother promised to make more than 100 red hats for the Buddhas if she gave birth to a son. Once in a while another woman would dutifully pray in front of a statue, look furtively around to see if anyone were watching, then snatch a red hat and hurry out of the temple, hoping that another woman's good luck might rub off on her.

Nine months after my father's visit, mother gave birth to her third baby. Both Auntie Chus attended her. There was much hustling about, murmuring and comings and goings. It seemed a lot of fuss about another baby.

Because our temporary rooms stood above the ceremonial hall where the family paid their respect to Buddha, mother was moved to the rickshaw house for the birth, since the blood accompanying childbirth was connected to bad omens.

I watched in apprehension as the flurry of people came and went from the rickshaw house. Even Sio Ying was present for the event. When the doctor came out with a dour expression, she glided up to him and the two exchanged words. Her smile, when she turned toward me, reminded me of a paper dragon.

The following day, Auntie Chu took my hand, led me into the rickshaw house and up the wooden stairs to see the baby. "You have a baby brother. His name will be U-Ching." (Pei Ching Jr.)

The curtains were drawn closed. Mother, covered with a quilt, lay on a small bed on the far side of the room. I peered closely at the new baby in the small wood cradle, then turned to Auntie Chu. "His face is sooo white," I said. "He's big, not like Fung Child."

"Hush, Tek Child. Don't bother your mother. She's very

tired. Come, Second Auntie Chu will comb your hair and braid it with a red thread."

"Not red! I hate red! Mother always makes me wear red threads in my hair."

"Yes, yes," she said, ushering me out of the room.

" I'd like many colors."

"Second Auntie Chu will braid your hair on one side with silver, blue, and pink threads. Then she can decorate your chignon on the other side with a jade butterfly and a ruby flower pin."

Excited with this prospect, I forgot about my new "white" baby brother.

Chapter 4

After the birth of my baby brother, Second Auntie Chu and I grew closer. In those days most well-to-do Chinese women were confined to their family compounds, and pretty women never went out on the street alone.

"I'm going shopping," Second Auntie Chu said, as she stood before me in a hand-embroidered Chinese dress with lace-trimmed sleeves. "Your mother said you may go with me." Instead of a servant accompanying her, I had become her number one escort. The servants might gossip about where she went, or what she did, or how long she stayed out, but she was safe with me.

Without any hesitation I joined her. Our rickshaw took us down Nanking Road to the large Cantonese owned department stores, Wing On, Sun Sun, and Sincere. Stores towered like cliffs on either side of the street. Open-fronted Chinese shops selling duck feet, fruit, fish, or clothing snuggled in small side streets behind the large imposing English-style stores. Alighting from our rickshaw, Auntie and I stood hand in hand on the corner of Nanking and Chekiang Roads amidst the jostling crowd in front of the Sincere

Department Store with its arched windows and entryway. Every surface on the outside of the building was decorated.

Auntie pointed to the columns that graced the sides of the arch on the first floor. "Those are called Corinthian columns. See those scrolls at the top. They're called friezes."

I gazed upward and saw that at each floor eaves extended over the rectangular windows from the third floor on up to the sixth floor, and a tall spire stretched to heaven from the top of the building.

"If you come with me, you must promise never to tell where we went." Second Auntie Chu's sparkling eyes danced with excitement as I readily said, "I won't tell!" We walked past the palm trees growing in brown tubs outside Sincere's Department Store and rode the elevator to the roof garden theater to watch a Shanghai local musical show. I was dazzled. The only other show I had seen was the performance of the Daikoo girls in Fung Tien.

Back out on the street, my Auntie's cheeks glowed, not from make-up, but from the admiring glances of the actors leaving the building and from other men as well. In her traditional dress she was a sharp contrast to women we passed dressed in cheongsams, who had bobbed hair and powdered faces. The sweet odor of a foreign women's perfume mixed with the stink of gasoline fumes made me sneeze. And while we waited for the electric streetcar to take us to our next destination, I pointed to a Caucasian woman with bright red-dyed hair.

"She looks so funny," I said to Second Auntie.

"Hush." She pushed down my arm. "Don't point at the foreigners."

The red-headed woman took a tall naval officer's arm, and together they sauntered over to a rickshaw, where the two tried to squeeze onto the one seat by her sitting on his lap. The rickshaw man shook his head, thrust out his hand and demanded, "More money! More money!"

The naval officer pushed the man's hands away from his immaculate white uniform, then dug into his pocket as he kept saying, "Okay. Okay. Take it easy." These explorations of Shanghai with Second Auntie Chu ended when I was ready to attend school. Since my father was still in the north, my Auntie's son recommended St. Mary's, a Catholic girl's school.

* * *

On the first day of school, mother and I entered the grounds with their lush green grass bordered by beds of flowers. I skipped along, happy to see the playground with the swings next to the classrooms. Abruptly I stopped, yanking my mother's hand.

"What's wrong Tek Child?"

"Look at the way the other girls are dressed," I whispered to her.

"It's a foreign school," she said. "It's all right for them to dress in westernized skirts and blouses."

I looked down at my long navy-blue brocade dress and hand-made embroidered shoes. I wanted to tell her that I felt like a country girl, but didn't dare.

Mother brushed her hand over my two tight pigtails that dangled down each side of my face. "You look very pretty."

I felt ugly.

Days passed and I grew more and more upset with my mother. When she came in our private rickshaw to pick me up after school, I was worried what the other girls would think of her half-bound feet, black skirt and gray top, and her face bare of make-up. Mother was only thirty-three years old, but I saw her as an ugly old woman.

One morning I pouted in front of the mirror as mother braided my hair. "Ouch. Ouch. Not so tight," I said, squirming on the wooden stool. "Why can't I have my hair cut the way the other girls do? Some of the girls have ribbons in their hair." I made a wicked face in the mirror. "My clothes are old, not like the other girls' dresses."

"You are not other girls. You are Wu child, daughter of Pei Ching. We dress like Chinese, not like foreigners."

I had no answer for her logic and would never think of contradicting her, but I itched to be like the other girls. "Can Auntie Yuk Ching pick me up today?" Auntie Yuk Ching had recently come to live with us permanently. "I want her to pick me up!"

"Why?" mother asked with a perplexed look.

"I just want her." I smiled inside, knowing I would get my way. Auntie Yuk Ching was younger than mother, dressed less severely, didn't have half-bound feet, and although she wasn't pretty, her presence would make a better impression on the other students.

Mother nodded. "All right. If that's what you want. Did you learn your lessons for the day?"

"I memorized their Lord's prayer in English as well as Chinese," I said with some pride. I spouted the prayer in English, which was gibberish to mother. The school was teaching me English, but no one at home could help me with the new language.

"I like the story Little Cucumber. This boy was the littlest of seven brothers. He was only as big as a cucumber, but he was the cleverest of them all. I like some of their Christian stories about Jesus, too. Why don't they tell stories about Buddha?"

"It's a Christian school," mother explained. "You learn about Buddha at home. You will grow up very smart learning both ways."

I sighed, wondering about this strange mix of ideas.

My background was very traditional in comparison to the other girls at the school. My parents had learned classical Chinese from private teachers, but had never attended school.

My family called the school the "foreign school" or "modern school." Just as China had to deal with dual beliefs so did I. During the school year, I fell ill with typhoid fever. Penicillin had not been discovered yet, and typhoid was often fatal. Mother was going to send a telegram to my father telling him to come home immediately, but before she could send the message, she received one from him saying he was ill. Hearing that, she didn't send her telegram. Apparently, she didn't want to worry him while he was ill.

She nursed me to recovery with the western medicine then available. "I want more to eat," I complained as she doled out a small portion of pork and vegetable soup.

After mother had left my room, I threw back my covers, ran to the kitchen, stepped on a small stool to reach the stove, and helped myself to a full bowl of rice and pork. When she caught me, I was just scraping the last bits of pork from my bowl. "See," I said. "I needed more food. I'm not sick anymore."

Mother frowned and walked me back to my room. At first I skipped along happy that I'd taken charge. Three steps later I was looking for the ma-tung.

After my relapse mother prayed for me in the Temple and changed doctors; the first man had been Western-educated and had told mother my relapse would be fatal. The second doctor treated patients with Chinese herbs. Dr. Chung was deaf, but had a reputation for healing typhoid patients.

"I don't like Dr. Deaf Chung," I whined. I made a face as mother tried to make me drink the bitter-tasting black liquid he'd prescribed. "I won't touch it."

"It isn't so bad," mother said. "You can take it with these lovely raisins. See?" She held out the bribe.

I wrinkled my nose. "Those aren't real raisins. You got them from the Chinese druggist."

"Be a good girl," Auntie Yuk Ching said, "and do what your mother says. The medicine will make you well."

I folded my arms across my chest and glared at them. "I won't drink it!"

Auntie Yuk Ching and mother looked at each other. Without warning, mother reached over and held my nose, and with Auntie Yuk Ching's help, she poured the foul mixture into my mouth. I kicked and cried, trying to push their hands away. By the time I swallowed the medicine, my face and clothes were black too. Auntie and mother cleaned me up and put me to bed.

Mother lay beside me weeping., "She's Pei Ching's heart, liver, and precious treasure," she said to Auntie. "How could I lose her?"

For me, the best part of my recovery was father's permanent return from the north. The Japanese were convinced they could not control Manchuria with General Zhang Zoulin alive. In June 1927 in Shenyang, a town not far from Fung Tien, as Zhang Zoulin was retreating in his private car on his private train, the Japanese blew up his train and blamed their action on Chinese bandits. With the Japanese assassination of Zhang Zoulin, father left his job, claiming illness.

While I helped mother unpack father's trunks, pictures of a beautiful woman floated to the floor. Mother picked them up and read one of the inscriptions: "With Love, Butterfly." Scornfully mother tossed the pictures back onto the floor and with a clank of force covered them with the ma-tung.

"So much for Miss Butterfly," she said.

Father took on life in Shanghai with the same drive and ambition that he had applied to the arsenal. When he embraced Shanghai, he also embraced his past, a past that included Sio Ying and Gun Yuen, their son.

Chapter 5

A perceptive change came over the Chus' household. My aunties and my mother laughed less, and frowns worked on everyone's faces. When father came into the house after one of his daily surveys for property around Shanghai, mother ran up to him. "We heard the Communists trade unions have taken over Chapei. There's fighting in the streets."

The Chus and mother encircled him, waiting for his response. "You're safe here, father said. "There's fighting only in the suburbs controlled by the Communists. Everything will be all right."

"How can you be so sure?" mother said. "Look what the Communists did in Hankou earlier this year. They slaughtered hundreds of wealthy businessmen."

"Yes, but that won't happen here. General Chiang Kaishek's army is on the move. He'll help us." He paused and added, "If he doesn't destroy us in the process."

"How can you say such things about Chiang?" Auntie Chu's son asked.

Father sat in his favorite chair in the Chu's center room

and unfolded his newspaper, ignoring the question. "I'm thinking of buying land in the French Concession."

"Is that where you were today? How did you get through?" Auntie Yuk Ching asked. "There are foreigner's gunboats anchored in the Whangpoo."

"Why don't you like Chiang?" Auntie Chu's son persisted pestering father.

His mother pushed him back and continued the barrage. "We heard barbed wire has been strung from North Railroad Station down through Hungjao Road to Siccawei, separating the French Concession and the International Settlement from our Chinese territory."

"It's not as bad as the rumors say." Father pointed to his paper. "Du Yuesheng has sided with the French Concession's Chief of Police to protect the foreign concessions against the Communists."

"But he controls the gambling and the opium trade in Shanghai," Auntie Chu said, wringing her hands.

"Exactly!" father said "Don't you think Du knows that his criminal enterprises would end if the Communists took control."

That silenced everyone, and father had his peace for a few moments.

But peace for Shanghai never really came. In March 22, 1927, Chiang Kaishek's gunboat passed the forty-five international nations' gun ships on the Whangpoo River. Less than a month later, on April 12th, Chiang's troops decimated the Communists. Afterward, during a three-week period, called "White Terror," Chiang's troops executed 12,000 supposed Chinese Communists. With this blood on his hands, Chiang Kaishek had taken over greater Shanghai, pleasing both Chinese leaders and foreign authorities.

Foreigners in Shanghai believed their city had survived because of the international gunboats on the Bund. But father insisted that it was the gangster, Du Yuesheng, who had saved the international sections. During this volatile time my father's wealth and his solid reputation protected our status. Because father had prospered during his time as Zhang Zoulin's chief of the arsenal manufacturing company, he was in a position to purchase land and build a house in the British, French, or Chinese areas. He bypassed the crowded, dirty, noisy Chinese section. The British section did not appeal to him, since its business center of tall commercial buildings stood near the Whangpoo River, and its residential area huddled far from the river, with little open land. He settled on the French Concession.

I walked proudly beside my handsome father as we explored the French Concession area to find just the right spot for our house. He strode with self-assurance, wearing the traditional long Chinese men's style gown with high collars and long sleeves. He swung his walking stick decorated with a silver-patterned ring as he went. Like a sturdy soldier, I measured my steps to his, keeping in his shadow, twirling the ivory-handled stick he had given me.

Each day we set out he turned to me and said, "Sit like a clock, and stand like a pine tree."

And I did.

Tek Ying and Father

After many days of searching, he found what he wanted—one and a half acres of land close enough to the city for convenience, but away from the smell and the noise. The following year he spent dealing with contractors and supervising work on the house. He didn't have an architect, but gave the contractor ideas about what he wanted in his Chinese modern house. He walked to the site every day to watch the workers measure, dig, mix cement, and pound nails as his house took shape.

Dozen of workers constructed the house by hand. Providing a firm foundation required many workers to tamp down the earth. They performed this task by building a rough, narrow, wooden rack about ten feet high on which four or five workers could stand. Inside the rack they laid a huge dead tree trunk supported by ropes. Each of the men standing on the rack held a rope, and in unison they pulled up on these ropes, lifting the trunk then dropping it onto the earth, tamping the soil solid and even.

The sweating men worked in relay teams, taking turns because of the weight of the tree trunk. They chanted rhythmically, "e-yo, e-yo, e-yo;" in between the "e-yos" they would toss out comments about girls who might be passing by. They chanted: "e-yo, e-yo, little sister's breast are big," or some other sexy remark. Young girls, who knew what was going on, tried to avoid the area where the "soil tampers" worked.

Father treated the workers in a friendly manner and sometimes ordered from nearby vendors extra nice dishes of pork or chicken for their lunch, which they normally couldn't afford.

As a result the workers were kind to me. They gave me a few bricks, some mortar and a trowel and showed me how to stack the bricks and cement them together. It didn't seem to matter to anyone that I was a mere girl. I was helping build my father's house on Du Ford Road.

The finished three-story house, garage, walks and

driveways and gardens formed a one-and-a-half acre compound. At first, only my father, mother, brother, myself, Auntie Yuk Ching and our eight servants occupied the house. Inside a cement-covered wall, tall pine trees hid the compound gate from the street. At one end of this wall hung a huge, double iron gate for cars to pass through. Two circular bronze plaques bearing the symbols for my father's name highlighted the gates. In one gate a high threshold and small door was cut out, where I would sometimes sit and count the number of passers-by on the quiet street. Cars driving through the main gate went to the front of the house or passed under an arched grape arbor to a large cement area by the garage.

Characters Representing Wu Pei Ching's House

Every week for a month father brought home a different car. "Ride in this one," he said to mother.

"I can't stand it," she said. "They all make me sick."

"I'll find one that doesn't make you carsick."

Finally, he bought a black Buick. Did mother give in or was this car really more comfortable for her? The Buick had luxurious fittings and a small jump seat set against the back of the chauffeur's seat. For the back seat father ordered small vases mounted above the green satin curtained windows. These always held sweet smelling hyacinths, his favorite flower.

The hyacinths grew in our greenhouse, which harbored many exotic plants. Immaculately trimmed trees ran along the back fence, with a row of porcelain stools lining the edge of the walk-way. Flowering peach and plum trees graced the manicured lawn.

Across from the garden at the front of the house, stood two columns on each side of broad stairs that led up to the two doors opening into the main hall. Here family ceremonies took place. The hall was furnished with a large circular table and behind it stood a carved sideboard holding decorative vases and candlesticks. To the left of the hall lay a living room furnished in Western style, and to the right a living room in Chinese decor. Peking wool rugs partially covered the gleaming polished wood floors.

These rooms stood empty most of the time, for the family preferred gathering in the smaller less formal rooms where the atmosphere was more relaxed, making it easier to chat and laugh. But father liked the elaborate rooms and would pace through them, taking pleasure in what he had built. He quoted Confucius: "By building the house on a sound foundation, the world is made secure."

To take care of the house and the premises, a large staff lived in the servants' quarters located behind the garage. This building and the kitchen were separated from the main house by the glass-covered greenhouse and washroom. Here mens' and womens' clothes were washed separately; they were hung on separate clotheslines to dry, for mixing them was considered disgraceful. Even more discretely, the servants hung women's undergarments out of sight in the back of the house.

Father spent lavishly on the furnishings of the house and he wanted mother to do the same. One day he filled his gown with paper money, marched into mother's bedroom and flung the bills on her bed, shouting, "Here, I have plenty. Go spend it!"

She cringed back in the bed, crying, without touching the money.

"Go shopping!" father said. "You have a big new house. Enjoy it."

"Tek Child's father, you are too generous. Maids do the cooking, washing and cleaning. All other responsibilities are done by the servants. Even U-Ching has a nanny."

"That's as it should be. Enjoy my wealth. Money is to be used."

Despite my father's tirade, later that same day I saw mother cleaning the depressions in the carved rosewood furniture with a chopstick covered with an oiled cloth. She scowled in concentration. Not until the mail came did she rest from her task. Upon opening a letter from Wu Sih, she clasped her hands together and smiled. "Tek Child, we are to have visitors. My sisters, your Third Auntie and Fourth Auntie, and their children have accepted our invitation. They're eager to see our new house."

My country cousins, five-year-old Ah-Ming, and her four-year-old brother, Luno, were very curious about our house. They gazed in awe at the large rooms and ornate decorations. Acting very adult, although I was only seven years old, I showed them the bathroom with the white porcelain basin, bathtub and toilet. Their eyes grew wide. Water coming from a faucet was a wonder; in the country they carried water into the house from a well or from the lake, bucket by bucket.

"Look at this!" My cousins dangled their hands into the toilet, thinking it was a basin for washing their hands. Before I could explain, Luno cried out, "Where's the ma-tung? I have to go potty."

"No. No." I scolded with my adult voice and showed both

of them how the new bathroom worked. It's not surprising that the Chinese still call a faucet, "Tsu-lai-zsu," meaning "The water comes out by itself."

To celebrate both our new house and the Chinese New Year, we had a big party with my mother's cousins and my father's younger brother and sister, all from Wu Sih, as well as my Auntie Chus and their son. With them and my father's many friends from Shanghai we had a full house. The household help spent days preparing food and making decorations.

Ah-Ming and I compared our new dresses, twirling in front of a mirror in my bedroom. "See," I said, "my mother even made me new shoes." I lifted one leg and pointed my toe showing off mother's embroidery.

"I have new underwear," Ah-Ming said, lifting her gown above her waist.

Luno who sat on the bed watching, giggled. In a flash Ah-Ming turned on her brother. "You have new underwear too." She tried to pull up his gown, but he squirmed free.

"Everyone has new clothes," he shouted as he ran out of the room. "It's New Years!"

The day of Chinese New Year, we children–myself, Ah-Ming, and Luno–dashed to the main hall to greet the new arrivals. Out of respect we dutifully kowtowed, kneeling down, stretching out our arms, and touching our foreheads to the floor. Luno was too young to understand his role in this custom. He giggled, played peek-a-boo and made faces despite his mother's scolding. When we jumped up from our kowtow positions, our relatives and friends pressed the customary gift of money folded into red paper into our waiting hands. This red paper money symbolized good fortune. I tried to maintain a serious demeanor, but Ah-Ming's and Luno's smiles split their glowing faces. While we entertained ourselves greeting the guests, the adults drifted off into the main rooms.

Mother, who usually dressed in plain, old-fashioned clothes, dressed elegantly. Her fur-lined deep-sea-blue brocaded top was beaded around the neck and edges of the sleeves. Below this Chinese style jacket, she wore a long red silk pleated skirt decorated with multi-pink embroidery. Fresh strung pearls in a flower design with dangling pearls hanging down one side covered her chignon. In the center of her chignon shone a red ruby in the shape of a good luck sign, with pearls surrounding the ruby and a jade hairpin inserted next to it. Flower-shaped diamond earrings gleamed in her ears. I gasped at her unexpected loveliness. Would father tell her how grand she looked?

When Sio Ying arrived dressed in an embroidered white round-cornered jacket, I could see mother wilt. Sio Ying's hips swayed seductively with her mincing steps as she entered our house. She was a delicate courtesan with a false smile. Was the smile sexual for father?

She was free to come and go in our house. Since her husband and mother-in-law had passed away, father rented a house for her and her two children. Now he supported Sio Ying, her son, Gun Yuen, who was my father's child, and Sio Ying's daughter by Yang, Ah-May. Gun Yuen called my father "cousin" in public, and used the term "Papa" only in private. He was a tall, handsome boy, and I wished I could tell people he was my brother.

On this day the swirling festivities allowed no time for reflection about relationships. Sio Ying as well as her children were welcome. All the chairs and tables were decorated with red embroidered silk covers, for red signified happiness. Four fireplaces crackled on the first and second floors. Small brass warming stoves, called "huo guo"–hot pots– glowed in the centers of each dining table. Trays around the base of the pots contained delicious and symbolic food. Bamboo shoots stood for progress and prosperity; crescent-shaped egg dumplings symbolized gold; transparent noodles suggested silver money; spinach symbolized closeness and love, and fish symbolized a surplus of man's needs. There was shark fin soup, sea cucumber, stuffed duck, whole chicken, roasted pork, platters of ham, and shrimp.

Heaped trays of sweet bean buns standing for harmony and good feelings and New Year's cakes symbolizing sweetness stood on each table. The tradition of nine dishes, meaning "forever," or ten dishes, meaning "perfection" was also honored.

We had no lack of food. The land father had bought for grandmother in Wu Sih furnished tons of rice for our Shanghai home. We never lacked meat. Tenant farmers on the land, under the management of Lok Hsiao-ming, raised the pigs, which were butchered, cured and delivered to our kitchen storage area.

Everything about the celebration signaled hope and happiness, for this day was everyone's birthday. No matter what day we were born we turned a year older on New Year's day. No one worked on the first day of the New Year, not even servants. Sweeping was not done, for this would signify that money was being swept out. Knives weren't used, because cutting was deemed to be a bad omen. No money was ever exchanged on this day. If someone owed you money, you would wait until the following day to collect.

Prior to the New Year period, friends and relatives would send packages to each other through their servants. When a servant from another house knocked on our back door, one of our servants opened it up.

"I've brought the house of Wu gifts from the house of Chang," the servant from Chang announced. Stepping forward into our house, he put the basket of fruit, a whole ham, a trussed up live chicken and candy on the floor. He opened a small rosewood box that contained his master's card and the house of Wu's address and placed the box on a table next to the door. A tip for the servant would be placed inside the box.

Our servant looked at the gifts and went in search of mother. Upon returning with her orders to refuse most of the gifts, our servant exclaimed, "Our Tai-Tai says the gift is too much! She cannot accept such generosity."

"Yes. Yes. Your mistress must accept. My master wishes much luck to the Wu family."

Our servant peered into the basket. "My mistress will take the ham" he said, lifting out a large gift wrapped ham, but nothing else. "All else is too much."

"No! You must take the entire basket." The other man pushed the basket into our servant's hands.

"I can't. Don't you see?" he said, pushing the basket back toward the other man. "My mistress and master would be angry with me for accepting such a huge gift."

The two servants argued, pushing the basket back and forth between them while the live trussed-up chicken clucked madly.

"I can't accept 'no' for an answer. Do you want me to lose face?"

"All right! I'll take the ham and fruit, but that's all." Our servant pushed the man out the door after relieving him of those parts of the gifts he would accept for our house. Happy that he had at last done his mistress's biding, he turned his back on the closed door and walked away with a grin on his face.

The closed door opened again soundlessly. Chang's servant tossed the trussed-up live chicken inside the room, grabbed the box with his tip inside and retreated from our compound. This game was carried out in every household with servants fighting not to accept too much from the other party.

* * *

By summer due to China's political situation and father's generosity, thirty family members and servants, including twelve children, spilled into our many rooms. The Japanese continued their domination of Manchuria. The Communists and remaining warlords fought against them. Relatives fled the Japanese and the two warring Chinese armies, causing father's safe compound to swell with family members.

The entire population of the Shanghai area grew. Hongkew, although part of the International Settlement, became the poor foreigners' section. Many pro-Japanese demonstrations took place in Hongkew because of its large Japanese population. In the filthy alleyways of Nantao, begging was a way of life. Between these downtrodden parts of Shanghai lived well-to-do foreigners and Chinese. Like many others, father's house was protected in the French Concession.

Siblings and Cousins On The Steps of the Wu House

Within this safe compound, children's laughter echoed through the house and grounds. Now my two girl cousins and ten boy cousins stomped through the area. The two bicycles the servants rode to deliver and pick up packages were the focus of excitement. Very early in the morning, before the servants set off on their errands, a couple of the boys got up and slipped outside to be the first ones on the bicycles. Soon the others got into the spirit of the game. The boys took turns, yanking the bikes away from each other. If one of the younger boys won a bike that was too big for him, he would still climb on, fall off, jump on again and fall again. During their zigzag rides, they bumped into the porcelain stools lining the garden and broke them and even destroyed father's favorite rose bed. As their voices grew louder, one of the servants ran outside. "Hush! You will wake Big Uncle. Stop!" He ran after the boys, his apron flapping, his cap askew on his head. "You'll see. Big Uncle will come out and give you the back of his hand." The boys ignored him. The servant threw up his hands and went back inside, muttering to himself.

Later father viewed the damage to the yard and garden, turned, beckoned for the gardener and pointed to the porcelain stools. "Replace those with ceramic ones."

The gardener shook his head. "I don't think it will work. Your nephews are wild with bike fever. Ceramic breaks too."

"We'll try. If that doesn't work..." Father's eyes strayed over the area. "If not, leave the area void of anything breakable."

"Your garden will not hold up to the boys' search for crickets," the gardener said.

Father nodded. "Do your best. Youth cannot always be confined."

Neither father nor my Aunties were able to stem the boy's enthusiasm for catching crickets. Each child had his own ceramic container for crickets and each was eager to keep for himself the crickets he found. They hid their containers under their bed and fed the captured crickets scraps of food. Sometimes the older boys pitted two crickets against each other, urging them on by tickling them with sticks of straw.

Unfortunately for the garden, the real fun for my cousins was listening for and catching the crickets. Quietly before dawn they would go outside, strain to hear the chirping crickets, and head in their direction. Each child would run for a spot, turning over pots and plants, scratching in the dirt under trees and along walls, and furiously digging until he found the cricket. The boys were like mice scurrying around in the dark. Little by little pots were disarranged—some broken—and the garden riddled with holes and upturned plants.

Again and again father conferred with the gardener. But after each meeting both left shaking their heads.

On warm summer evenings as the family gathered outside, sitting in rattan chairs, fanning themselves, chatting and enjoying cold watermelon, my boy cousins sat nearby, straining to hear the chirping crickets. When their eyes turned toward the sound, you'd know they were hatching plans for their morning hunt. The next morning into the house they tramped, dirty from head to toe from digging in the garden. Their angry mothers met them at the door.

Although father's acreage and beautiful house took a great deal of punishment, both afforded the family much pleasure, especially during watermelon time. Summertime brought the sweet taste of this fruit. But beside enjoying the treat, Chinese regarded watermelon as therapy to bring down fever. Chinese did with watermelon what Westerners do when they drink liquids to control a fever.

Every family kept watermelon on hand during the summer. Street vendors, carrying the melons in two flat baskets suspended from each end of a bamboo pole balanced across their shoulders, strolled down the street calling, "Selling sweet watermelon—guaranteed."

When a customer approached to bargain, the vendor

said, "You want to be sure it's good melon. I'll cut a square piece out of the melon for you to taste, then you will know you're getting a good one."

"No. I have to pay extra for that," the potential customer said.

"You can buy it as is, but how will you know your watermelon will be sweet?"

"Agreed. But I'll pay extra only if the melon is sweet."

"You'll see." The vendor cut out a piece of melon. "It will be so sweet you will want to buy more than just one."

Since so many people lived in our house, father ordered as much as 800 to 900 pounds of watermelon from a wholesaler, not a street vendor. The delivery brought mounds of melons, more than any market display. The servants carried the melons, one by one, into our living room, where they stacked them under the large rosewood table in the center of the room to keep them cool.

On delivery day the other children swarmed about the truck to help the servants unload the wagon. Two of my older boy cousins hauled a melon off the truck, started up the broad stairs guarded by two columns and staggered into the house with it. At just the right moment, my cousins looked at each other, nodded and plopped the melon onto the tile floor—an instant feast.

In the compound we had our own life and only occasionally would news from the outside world filter in to us. For as always, father protected his small realm. But we responded with ambivalence to the news that the international troops were departing from Shanghai. Du retained his power, and Chiang Kaishek began his reign of taxation and corruption. There were no winners for the long term. Wealth and gaiety juxtaposed against poverty and corruption in Shanghai.

However, I wasn't interested in politics that first summer in our new house, for the Kitchen god brought me deep sadness.

Chapter 6

1929

It was June. We had been in our house six months. New growth sprouted in the trees, flowers bloomed, and we relished the special fresh peaches from Longhua, the same town where father had worked at the arsenal factory many years before. Out of affection for our father, the mid-wife who had aided in his birth brought the peaches to us.

One day after lunch mother became extremely ill.

"Let me rest," she said, "then I'll feel better. I've only eaten too many peaches."

But after several days of her continued and worsening pain, father insisted she go to the hospital. He waited for the German doctor's opinion. "She has a twisted intestine. If you'd brought her in immediately, we might have been able to operate. Now, it would be very risky, but without surgery, she will die."

"No operation," mother said. "I want my whole body intact when I die. I want only to go home to die." Six days later she was released from the hospital after the doctor gave her an injection to prolong her life for a short time.

We moved her bed out of her room and into the Chinese living room. I stood in the far corner of the room, while mother grasped Auntie Yuk Ching's hand and whispered just loud enough for me to overhear. "I swear I will come back as a ghost and choke Sio Ying. All these years she has tried to take Tek Child's father from me. She corrupts Tek Ying's father's thoughts."

Why did she rave on so about Sio Ying?

Father came into the room, leaned over mother's bed and asked, "Does anyone owe you money that you want to collect?"

Mother waved her hand feebly. "Let it go. That's for the next life." She looked paler and sicker with every word.

"Do you have anything you want to tell me?" father asked.

For a moment she seemed startled, then slowly shook her head.

I fled to family members gathered in the backyard. My aunties, a servant and I prayed to the gods for a miracle and burned incense and paper money to strengthen our prayers. In the midst of our prayers, one of my uncles rushed out of the house, grabbed me by the arm and led me back inside to my mother's bedside. Too late. My uncle pressed on my shoulder so I would kneel next to U-Ching at the side of mother's deathbed.

I stared at mother lying there on the bed in the middle of the ornate room, so still, so quiet. Where was her spirit? Mother would no longer be here for me. This was much worse than Fung Child's death. All the naughty things I had done exploded like fireworks inside my head. Through the years I had ignored her chiding words. I looked at her passive gray face, but heard her scolding voice, "You'll be sorry—after I die you'll get a stepmother's fist when you don't behave." I crouched down at her deathbed and wailed, "Now, I'll get the fist from a stepmother."

My father hugged me to him. The salt of his tears and mine mingled as I pressed my cheek against his neck. "Don't worry little tiger," he said, "I love you. Dada will always be with you."

While my father held me, U-Ching bobbed up from his kneeling position and walked about mother's bed, shaking his finger at her body. "See? Look at you. That's what you get for eating too many peaches."

My uncle came forward and took hold of the three-year-old and hushed him. But relatives, now gathered against the far wall of the room, nodded and muttered amongst themselves. "See? Such behavior! That proves it."

I didn't know what they meant.

I stayed out of everyone's way and walked around the house watching the practical arrangements that were being made to show our respect for mother. Custom demanded an initial seven day mourning period, but before it could begin, her body had to be preserved from the summer heat. Father ordered blocks of ice to be placed under mother's deathbed while he made the necessary preparations. The melting water ran across the floor as though mother's blood were seeping out.

To ready mother for her coffin, tailors came to the house and sewed through the night to make the seven pieces of special clothing she would wear–all pure silk of brilliant colors—shocking pink, blue, purple, turquoise, light green— colors not usually worn in those days, and certainly never worn by my mother. Each layer of the quilted silk-wool outer garment was lined, and in a matter of hours the clothing was ready.

"Come, Tek Child," Auntie Yuk Ching said to me while I sat outside watching my cousins play. "You must be clothed in the seven layers of garments that your mother will wear."

Because I was small and short, I stood on a stool as my aunties fitted each layer on my small body. Standing with my arms outstretched, I felt surrounded by the sound of my praying and weeping relatives. Like flowing blood, perspiration ran down my back and legs as layer after layer of clothing was slipped over my head and fitted. My arms ached and I began to cry.

"Why must I do this? Can't you measure and then sew the clothes?"

"No," Auntie Yuk Ching said. "It's important that you warm the garments so your mother will not feel the cold in her dark coffin."

I bit my lower lip and stood like a pine tree as my father had taught me.

Mother's red silk skirt and rose-colored shoes from our housewarming celebration became part of her death clothing. A large pearl had been sewn on the headband she wore. This pearl and those sewn on each corner of her sleeves, on both sides of her skirt, and on the top of each shoe were to provide a glow so she wouldn't have to walk in the dark. In each hand she held a crescent-shaped piece of gold to insure she would not be poor in the other world.

Father purchased a red embroidered hooded cap from a store that sold funereal items. The hood hung down to cover mother's face, and my Auntie cut out an oval piece to show her face. The family would keep the cut-out material for good luck. After my mother was completely dressed, she was placed in her coffin, covered with a quilted silk wool embroidered blanket. The coffin was closed.

For seven days the coffin lay in the upper half of our ceremonial hall on whose walls hung white satin scrolls of consolation sent by relatives and friends. White curtains draped from the ceiling on each side of the coffin afforded a place behind which women family members mourned. Their cries and wails echoed from behind these curtains. White candles and incense burned constantly on a table in front of the coffin. Members of the family dressed in white.

My brother, U-Ching, and I wore head coverings with a

burlap flap hanging down to our noses. Pieces of burlap covered our shoes. He and I knelt by the coffin most of the day. My knees hurt and my back was sore. I tried to act like a pine tree, but often I gasped, and my dried salty tears plastered my cheeks. U-Ching fidgeted as we sat on the floor next to the coffin. We seldom spoke to each other as we ate our meals of tasteless bowls of rice the maids brought us.

"Where did mother go?" he asked me.

I shrugged.

"What will happen now?"

I shrugged.

"Talk to me Big Sister," he cried and reached out and grabbed my arm.

"It will be all right. Father will take care of us."

"Why do we have to kneel here all day? I want to go play."

"It's our duty to mother. You don't want to make her spirit angry do you?"

U-Ching sniffled. The whispering servants stood across the room watching us. His nanny scolded him for not being brave.

Friends and relatives came to pay their respects, and we gave each a white sash to wear. Handing it to them would mean giving them bad luck, so we dropped the sash on the floor in front of them. They then picked it up and tied it around their waists.

At the end of seven days, my mother's coffin was moved from our house to the Pin Yee Kwon located in a nearby suburb. According to Chinese custom, if the wife died before the husband, she could not be buried in the ground; she had to wait for his death. Until that time, the wife's coffin remained in this special house—Pin Yee Kwon—where a single room was set aside for her coffin. When the husband died, the wife and husband could be buried in the ground together. Some families who couldn't afford one room shared a room. The family paid an annual rental fee.

It was unbearably hot the day we left mother's coffin at the Pin Yee Kwon, and my stomach churned. On the way home, I sat in the back seat of our car tightly holding my mother's "spirit seat," a small block of wood carved with mother's name. Her "spirit seat" would hang with those of my grandparents and great-grandparents in a small wooden house in the corner up next to the ceiling of our Chinese living room. Normally it was the custom that the son held the "spirit seat." Instead, father had me hold it. Was this because I was the oldest or because mother loved me best?

Suddenly without warning, Ah-Bin, our chauffeur, yanked the Buick's steering wheel, swerving the car away from a coolie pulling his wares down the road. Ah-Bin braked, stopping with a jerk. I gaped at a blood-covered coolie sprawled in the road ahead of us. His wood-laden cart was askew, and the frayed rope he'd been pulling lay at his feet. When the rope broke, he'd fallen on the narrow, bumpy road in front of our car. Only bad things seemed to be happening.

When our car pulled into the driveway at our house, I couldn't make my legs move. I pushed myself off the seat and tried to stand, but my legs were wobbly. My uncle carried me into the house. He tried to stand me on a chair, but my legs collapsed under me. I was utterly miserable. Even though I was trembling and crying, uncle said, "Stop pretending! The day is over. Your duty is done."

Auntie Yuk Ching understood my feelings and put her arms around me. She tried to comfort me by telling me stories and giving me sweet treats. After a while I felt better, went up to father's room, stood in front of the long mirror next to his armoire and stared at my image. "Who am I?" I asked out loud. "Why did my sister and mother die on me?"

During the sad and empty days that followed, Auntie

Yuk Ching tried to comfort me. But when I heard the other families laughing and chatting in the back rooms, I ran to the western living room, buried my head in the couch and sobbed until the silk embroidered pillows were damp. "Mother! Mother! Why did you leave me alone? I want you to come back."

After the funeral, Father left the house often. One night I couldn't stand it any longer without him. I called him at the *Yao-Chih*. "You said you'd always be with me. But you aren't. You're never home any more."

I heard his heavy sigh, but he came home. Whenever he left the house to be with friends, I called him. Often I overheard them asking, "Will you be going home to nurse your daughter tonight?"

Even after the initial seven day mourning period for my mother passed, many customs still had to be observed. For forty-nine days after mother's death, family members could not visit anyone for fear of bringing bad luck. Each seventh day of the forty-nine, monks came to our house to pray for mother to insure that she would be able to survive the journey through the underworld. During those days children in the family wore white clothing, and girls even wore white yarn flowers in their hair. After forty-nine days children could wear gray garments with white binding.

"Why do I have to wear these white shoes with their soft cotton soles?" I asked Auntie Yuk Ching. "I like my other shoes better."

"Your mother will slip while walking in the other world if you wear leather soled shoes," she said.

"Everything is different now that she's gone."

"Tek Child, these customs are important. They remind us that the household is in mourning. You are showing respect to your dead mother."

Father took a different view of life and death and intervened on our behalf. "I don't want people to feel sorry or sad for my children. They need to get back to a normal routine," he said to Auntie. "Let them wear black or navy blue instead of the funereal white. It won't make that much difference."

For a while after mother's death, I slept with father in his large bed. Normally, I would fall asleep long before he came to bed, but I loved the feel and smell of his covers about me. One night I awoke in the darkened room to strange noises. Someone was giggling. It was Sio Ying! I pulled the sheet over my face and feigned sleep, but my heart pounded. The laughter and throbbing of the mattress went on for a long time.

When I awoke the following morning, both Sio Ying and father were gone. The sheets didn't smell or feel the same. I gathered the sheets into a ball and threw them on the floor. "Sio Ying, I hate you!" I ran into my room and slammed shut the connecting door to my father's room. Nothing was the same since mother had died.

Chapter 7

After mother's death, Auntie Yuk Ching took charge of the house. Her first job was to get me back in school. Before mother died, she had chosen another Catholic girls' boarding school. When I visited this school with Auntie, I was pleased to notice that the playground was very large.

The Sisters greeted us warmly. "You'll make new friends here," the Sister said. She asked me questions about reading and writing, turned to Auntie and said, "We'll put her in the second grade."

Auntie turned to me. "Do you think you will like it here?"

I immediately answered, "Yes."

The following week off I went to board at the school. I was assigned a bed in a huge hall occupied by thirty other young girls. On the first morning while it was still dark outside, I heard footsteps. A Sister yanked aside the curtain surrounding my bed and shook me. "Six o'clock! Time to get up." Her stern face reminded me of a hooded falcon, and I cringed back into the bed.

"Come now. Up with you. Mustn't be lazy," she said and marched off to her next victim.

I stumbled to the wash room. Barely dipping my hands into the icy water, I dabbed at my face. None of the girls spoke, but hurriedly dressed and made their beds. I'd never made up a bed before. Sniffling, I watched the others and tried to mimic them. Finally too hungry to care about the lumpy and wrinkled bed, I began to try to get dressed, but I had never dressed myself without the help of a maid. I couldn't ask one of the other girls. They had all left for breakfast. Hurriedly I followed with my cheongsam half-buttoned and my hair dangling about my face.

After breakfast we students attended classes or studied; then we ate a brief lunch between more classes. Just before bedtime, we were allowed to go outside to walk, but not to play. While I stood in a corner of the play yard, shivering in the freezing cold, the other girls walked back and forth as if they were performing a ritualistic dance. In pairs or threes or fours they walked forward toward the fence, then upon reaching it, instead of turning around to walk back again, they walked backward.

When Auntie Yuk Ching came to visit, bringing chocolate and biscuits, I cried, "I want to go home."

"It's only because the school is new. Look what I brought you from your father," she said, handing me a package. Inside was a green satin hat with matching flowers on one side. I couldn't wear pink or red because I was in mourning.

I wore that hat every day, pulling it down over my forehead to hide my tear-swollen eyes and my unkempt hair. But nothing comforted me. Finally, I wrote father: "I can't stand the life here. I want to kill myself."

Auntie said that when father read my letter, tears came to his eyes. He shouted, "Bring that child back here right away. What were we thinking? She's only eight years old and no longer has a mother." Within ten days I returned home.

Now my studies continued at home with my four older cousins under the tutelage of Miss Chang, who had moved into our home. The middle room on the third floor, where pictures of my grand and great-grand parents hung, became our classroom. Our days were scheduled as though we were in regular school. Father ordered a blackboard and small square tables, and Miss Chang sat at a large desk in front of the board. The eyes of our ancestors looked down upon us, watching us work our lessons, so we resisted the temptation to tease each other or giggle while we worked.

One day while we were at recess playing *Tic-chien-tze*, a game played with a coin with a hole in the center through which a split-shafted feather had been sewn, Auntie Yuk Ching took me aside. "You and U-Ching are going with me to visit Miss Chu after school." Miss Chu was the head nurse Auntie had become friendly with when my mother was in the hospital. By now I was quite used to these afternoon visits, so I nodded absentmindedly and went back to the game, kicking the feathered coin into the air with one foot and trying to catch it with either foot. Instead it landed on my forehead, and I laughed at the way I had won the game.

That afternoon U-Ching and I followed Auntie into Miss Chu's austere hospital living quarters. We smiled politely at Miss Chu and thanked her as she gave us chocolates. U-Ching was particularly fond of the small paper bird she gave him. While we enjoyed our sweets, Auntie chatted with Miss Chu. "The children have been telling their father how much they like you, Miss Chu," Auntie said. "Their father would like you to come to dinner next week. We are having a small gathering of friends." When Miss Chu accepted the invitation, Auntie Yuk Ching's face lit up with more than normal pleasure.

The party had grown in number despite Auntie Yuk Ching's efforts to keep it small. U-Ching and I waited in restless anticipation the night of the dinner and watched from the Chinese living room as guests were welcomed into the main hall. Sio Ying, as usual and much to Auntie Yuk

Ching's disappointment, was also present. Sio Ying wore a pink jacket with wide flared three-quarter length sleeves that showed her entire upper arm when she gestured. At the party father smiled a pleasant greeting to the subtly dressed Miss Chu. "You must have a special way with children, for according to my sister, the children enjoy their visits with you."

Rapport seemed to be beginning between my father and Miss Chu. During the course of the evening, Auntie leaned over and whispered in my ear. "Would you like Miss Chu to become your new mother?" I smiled and nodded, yes.

Dinner came and went, and father and his friends gathered around the mah-jongg game-table. Sio Ying pulled up a chair next to father. She leaned close, allowing her arm to rub against him, patting his arm, smiling her dainty smile and clinging to his every word. More than once her eyes strayed to Miss Chu. Sio Ying's look was not pleasant, but could not be interpreted as inhospitable either.

Later, when Auntie eagerly asked Miss Chu about her feelings toward my father, she responded, "Your brother already has a girl friend!"

Our visits to Miss Chu's room ended abruptly.

Although Auntie had failed in her first match-making venture, she continued to try. Time after time, a casual visit ended with friends pulling out photographs of pretty women dressed up and smiling sweetly. They hoped to have father point to one and say, "Yes, I'd like to meet her." Father would call me to look at the photographs—a girl sitting in a high-backed peacock chair, her elbow resting on its arm, her hand touching her cheek, eyes lowered demurely and a coy smile on her face; another girl sitting on a sofa, her arms resting on silk pillows. Sio Ying was right there scanning the photos with me and frowning as she shook her head and murmured, "No, not that one—she's no good. She'd be a bad stepmother." That's all I needed. I said "no" to every woman.

After one of these occasions, as the family sat outside in the yard enjoying the sun, Auntie took me aside. "You're a silly girl for saying 'no' to all your father's prospects for marriage. You need a mother, but you'll never get one the way you've been acting."

I pouted and pulled away from her. I walked over to father, put my hands on my hips and announced, "I don't want to look at any more pictures. I want to go to a western restaurant."

"No. Not now. Maybe some other time."

I stamped my foot, burst into tears and ran over to a corner of the garden wall, hunching down and crying until I cried myself to sleep. Father had a manservant pick me up and carry me to bed. I awoke while he was carting me up the stairs. I screamed, "Put me back in the corner! I want to sleep there!" But he plodded on up the stairs. I wriggled, flailing my arms and scratching his face. Blood trickled down his chin, yet he never wavered in his duty to follow father's orders.

Another time during that same summer on a hot night when I didn't get what I wanted, I rolled myself up in a throw rug out in the garden. My cousins tittered and Auntie said, "You'll get sick." Then she and the others went back to their cool watermelon and comfortable chatter, completely ignoring me. I couldn't breathe, perspiration rolled down my neck and I itched from head to toe. Finally in a state of misery I unrolled myself and stared up into the bright night stars. Even the heavens were happy. Why wasn't I?

"She needs a stepmother," Auntie Yuk Ching muttered.

My father glanced my way. "You're only a tiger when you're in the cage, outside you're a quaking lamb."

While Auntie continued her search for a suitable woman for my father, our home teacher, Miss Chang, left to be married. My mother's cousin, Grandma Zee, began looking for a school for me and two of my cousins—the Zee sisters.

Grandma Zee was a countrywoman who'd had a special relationship with my mother. They'd shared secrets, and given and received sympathy. Now she did the same with me. I could count on her to soothe my hurts with my favorite foods or pleasant words, but her constant sad expression showed her feelings for my unhappiness in losing my mother.

The school she found for us was run by a young man who held classes in the living room of the house where he lived with his mother, sister, and nephew. He had only four students and was glad to enroll the three of us. We called it "The Seven Students" school.

This bright and handsome young teacher had a classical Chinese education and taught us in the same manner, exposing us to Confucius' sayings. Many nights I worked on memorizing Confucius' words so that I could write them out in class the next day. Father smiled and nodded his head approvingly while he listened to me repeating the wise words.

Grandma Zee's good heart didn't just respond to me; it reached out to all, including the *Ya Tua*, or slave girls, she bought from poverty-stricken families in Wu Sih.

At that time in China, poor families would sell their daughters, but never their sons, if they found they couldn't support them. The girls ranged in age from nine to fourteen. Once a buyer took the *Ya Tua* home, he or she could do whatever he wanted with her. If the girl did something wrong, even a minor thing, like serving too cold tea, she could be slapped, beaten or made to kneel down in a corner and go without food. If a *Ya Tua* were raped by the master or young master of the house, she, not he, would be blamed for what happened. A lucky *Ya Tua* might become his concubine. If that didn't take place, her jealous mistress might force the *Ya Tua* to commit suicide by hanging or by throwing herself off a bridge or into a well.

Grandma Zee felt that by buying the girls she could help them as well as their poor families. She taught them skills:

how to serve tea, help in the kitchen, sew and embroider. These skills could lead to the marriage Grandma Zee would later arrange. If the girls deserved to be punished, she talked to them and explained what they had done wrong; she never resorted to physical punishment.

Spring Orchid, one of Grandma Zee's *Ya Tuas*, benefited from her matchmaking. Spring Orchid's poor complexion prevented her from looking as lovely as an orchid, but her cleverness and quick mind made up for her appearance. The meals she prepared were tasty, her embroidery impeccable, and she even learned to read with help from the Zee sisters.

Grandma Zee was ecstatic when she found a suitable husband for Spring Orchid, a young man who worked in the Chinese section as a small shop owner. She bought Spring Orchid clothes for each of the seasons, and with the rest of the family's help, a dowry replete with linens and money was established.

When the Zee sisters and I teased Spring Orchid about her coming marriage, she blushed. "I don't want to leave," she cried. "You've treated me like one of the family."

I enjoyed being involved with all the preparation for Spring Orchid's departure into marriage and never dreamed that one day she would play a part with my leaving China. Oddly enough one of father's friends who came into our lives at about the same time as Spring Orchid's departure also played a part in my future.

Chapter 8

I first met Wong Yen Tai when father invited him to live at our house as a temporary guest, and I soon began to call him Uncle Wong. He was in Shanghai seeking to find an opportunity to set up a law firm. His wife, Hai Li, continued to live in Peking until he was settled.

"I hear you are learning English," Uncle Wong said to me when I interrupted father's and his conversation in the western-style living room.

"A little," I replied, hoping I wouldn't have to perform and speak a memorized piece.

"You don't know a culture until you know the language." I thought he was addressing me, but he looked at father.

"Yen Tai has been schooled in Germany and the United States as well as in the finest Chinese Universities," father said to me. "He speaks five languages."

Wong smiled, apparently pleased over father's bragging about him. "Your hospitality is most appreciated."

"Tell Tek Child some of the places you've been. One day she must travel and see the world."

"Most girls are more interested in fashion than history," Uncle Wong said. "What is your preference?"

"Fashion," I blurted out without hesitation.

"The world is quite different from China. But you have probably noted that from seeing the foreigners here. Even men have different styles. Take your father's short cropped hair," he said, turning to father. "A carry-over from your military days, I presume."

Father felt the top of his inch-long hair.

"It looks good on you," Uncle Wong continued, "but in many countries only prisoners wear their hair so short."

Father changed the subject. "Have you made contacts to help you in your business venture?"

"I thought I might see if any one needs legal letters written or other small services. That way I could establish myself gradually."

Father rose and went to the window. "See those trees located just inside our compound walls," he said to Yen Tai who joined him at the window. "Ever since I built this house the French Concession authorities have cited me for the fallen leaves on the street from those deciduous trees. During the fall months my servant rakes up the leaves early every morning, but to prevent leaves from remaining on the street at all times is an impossible task. So every fall, despite my diligence, I pay a fine for the wayward leaves."

Yen Tai smiled. "I think I can repay your hospitality. I'll write a letter to the French Authorities in French requesting leniency in the matter. I'll wager you won't ever be cited again."

The friendship between Wong Yen Tai and father grew. Soon father moved him into our western-style living room because it had a connecting bath. The room was transformed into a bedroom; the living room furniture was moved elsewhere, and a steward was assigned to take care of Yen Tai's needs. In time father decided to build an apartment for his friend over what had been the vegetable garden area. Underneath the apartment he built a double garage. He turned the old garage into quarters for Yen Tai's chauffeur and manservant. When the apartment was complete, father moved the pool table from our billiard room into the apartment's ground floor. In this room with its sofa, tables and chairs and billiard table, father and Yen Tai lunched together three times a week, talking and savoring special dishes the cook prepared just for them.

One day father asked me to join them because Uncle Wong hadn't seen me in a while. Uncle Wong intrigued me and I listened closely as he and my father talked.

"You do me great honor by building such an area for me," Uncle Wong said.

"The children have ruined the garden anyway. It was time to change things."

"You have been very successful in Shanghai," commented Uncle Wong. "I envy you your family. Aren't they a burden to you?"

Father brushed back his now long hair from his forehead and peered at his friend through his glasses. "One of my filial obligations is to create prosperity for my family. This insures the family's continuity."

"I have no family, only a wife," Uncle Wong said.

"Each member of a family is a pebble in the stream between ancestors and posterity. I am responsible for the acts of others in my household, and they are responsible for mine."

"You are true believer in Confucius," Yen Tai said. "I've seen too much of the world to believe in that philosophy."

"What do you believe in?" father asked.

"The art of the business deal," Yen Tai said and laughed.

"I appreciate that too. Besides my hotel, I found a business that will help my relatives. Within walking distance of my house there is a new housing development where over 100 Li (rental units) have been built. Do you know it?"

Yen Tai nodded, said nothing, but frowned.

Father continued, ignoring Yen Tai's reaction. "Hundreds of families live close by and use rice and oil every day. I saw that kind of shop would do well there. I leased three of the spaces, remodeled the interior walls into one large store and sent for three of my cousins to come to Shanghai to run the store, share the profits among themselves and live in the quarters above it. Business is good, and they are making a great deal of money. It gives me pleasure to stroll by the store and watch my cousins prosper."

"Have you been by there lately?" Yen Tai asked.

"Not for several months."

"I've heard rumors about your cousins. It's said they spend their money on other women, don't come home at night to be with their families, and they gamble. I tell you this as a friend, because if you are inclined to help them you are in for a difficult time."

Father scowled, but didn't respond. He had faith that his relatives were honorable men.

This information didn't dissuade father from other business deals. Later he bought land near the factory area of Xujiahui and built small, inexpensive housing units where workers could live. One of father's older servants asked father to provide him with a store outside these buildings, which he did. This ex-servant opened a small store selling items like candy, biscuits, rice cakes, matches, incense, toilet paper and other articles for everyday living. In lieu of paying rent, he collected the rent for father from the workers living in father's housing unit.

"A bank is just the thing," Yen Tai said. "I like my business ventures to be easy, with a quick return on my investment."

"Success is the effect of hard work," father said.

Father expected much of his family. "Being lazy is the worst quality a person can have," he would say. "It's not whether you're stupid or clever, but how hard you work."

However, despite their philosophical difference, he and Uncle Wong opened a bank together.

Since Uncle Wong was taking so much of father's time, I wanted to find out more about him. One day after Uncle Wong and father had gone out, I told Yen Tai's servant that I wanted to see his master's apartment. The servant opened the door for me. Instead of Chinese furnishings or even western furnishings, I saw black and white furniture set on a painted yellow floor. Was the room so odd because he'd seen the rest of the world?

After a while Yen Tai began bringing a woman to his apartment. She smelled of European perfume and dressed in brightly colored cheongsams. This mistress visited more and more often. One afternoon as the sun began to set, a car pulled into our compound, and out stepped a petite Chinese woman dressed in a sky blue cheongsam. Her hair was neatly tucked into a chignon, pearl earrings glinted in the fading light and a large diamond and jade ring twinkled with the last rays of the day's sun. Although she was tiny, her carriage was regal. From the amount of luggage the driver deposited in the hall, it was obvious the woman planned a long stay.

"I'm Mrs. Wong," the woman announced to our servant who ushered her into the ceremonial hall. Our servant bowed and ran to tell father of the arrival of Wong's wife.

While Hai Li Wong waited somewhat impatiently for her husband, I watched her from the living room where I'd been reading. When she spied me, she walked toward me, her high heels clicking on the shiny wood floor. Her dainty feet matched her figure. Apparently, foot binding had not distorted them. She cocked her head to one side and smiled at me. I rose from the large couch I'd been cuddled in and bowed, giving my name.

She nodded, saying, "The house of Wu has a lovely bright daughter. I will enjoy having conversations with you."

"You're staying with Uncle Wong, too?" I blurted out.

"I hear there is room enough for two in the apartment.

As long as my husband is welcome, I'm sure I will be welcome."

Before I could say anything further, father arrived, appearing cool and relaxed. "Welcome to my house, Mrs. Wong. Your husband will be here shortly. He had some dictating to finish with his secretary."

My mouth gaped open like a feeding fish. Secretary? Uncle Wong doesn't have a secretary here, I thought. Only his mistress comes and goes.

Yen Tai's servant gave a sign to father behind Mrs. Wong's back. What was going on at Yen Tai's apartment? Father invited Mrs. Wong to join him for tea and she graciously accepted. "Thank you for being such a generous host and acting so honorably while my husband attends to . . . his secretary . . . Is that what you said?"

"Tek Child, go outside and play," father ordered.

I wandered over to Uncle Wong's apartment. The door stood wide open; small suitcases with clothing peeking out the closed sides sat on the steps. Uncle Wong came out pushing his angry mistress in front of him. He never noticed me as he hustled the woman to his chauffeur-driven car.

Shortly after Hai Li moved in with her husband, Spring Orchid reappeared. Not knowing where else to turn when her husband died of typhoid, she returned to the house of Zee to take up her duties as a *Ya Tua* again. Since Hai Li needed a maid, Grandma Zee sent Spring Orchid to her.

During the time the Wongs lived in the new apartment on the compound, the required three-and-a-half years passed since my mother's death. This ended the official mourning period, which concluded with a final ceremony. For this occasion the tailor fashioned a long peach-colored brocaded cheongsam for me. I was eleven years old.

The ceremony took place at a shrine. We performed the ritual that would mark the time of my mother's passing to the other world. Using paper, workers had constructed an almost full-sized room furnished with a sofa, bed, dresser, and a life-sized maid. Next to the room a paper rickshaw man stood on alert by his rickshaw. These articles represented the earthly materials of mother's life going with her to heaven. While others were diverted, I crept into this paper room, opened a drawer in the paper chest and slipped in a paper handkerchief I had cut out for mother to take with her. Later, all the articles were set ablaze, giving them to my mother so she could live comfortably in the world waiting for her.

With the formal end of mourning for my mother, my life changed.

Chapter 9

1931

"The Zee sisters are going on to the Ming Li Girls' High School in the Chinese Territory," I said to father one night as the family ate at the large dining table. No one seemed to think this information was particularly important, but I continued. "I'd like to go too."

"Perhaps," father said.

"They're boarding, coming home once a week." I waited a moment for him to react. When he didn't, I continued pushing for my cause. "I can get a better education there."

Father put his chopsticks aside. "You may attend the school, but Ah-Bin will take you and pick you up everyday. You don't have to live at the school."

"You always say I'm a tiger only at home. I can be strong away from home."

He studied my face, a frown tracing his brow. "You haven't done well away from home."

"But I'm older now. I'm the oldest in the family and must set a good example."

Father nodded, then looked down at his rice bowl. "We will see."

Although I got my way, I had to put up with Ah-Bin picking me up on Saturday afternoons and driving me back to school Monday mornings to allow me some time at home. Among all the students at the school, I was the only one picked up by automobile. Ah-Bin had to maneuver the car up a narrow walled street, wide enough only for walkers or rickshaws. At the end of the road stood the school gate where I waited, anxious to climb in the car as quickly as I could. After I jumped into the back seat of the car, Ah-Bin backed slowly down the road. I scrunched down out of sight, hoping the students pressed against the wall to allow us to pass, wouldn't see me.

My two new friends, To Tsang and Illan Kwok made light of my being picked up by Ah-Bin. The three of us had met the first week of school, and as often happens we gained nicknames. To Tsang, a shy girl with large high cheekbones and a gentle look in her soft eyes, became Lucy, a name that stuck. Illan, an outgoing rebellious spirit, retained her name because she insisted. I became Anita. "Anita, chiquita, the banana girl," was a chant I hated. At least at home I was still Tek Ying.

Each weekend at home, Father welcomed me with a surprise. "Look what I bought," he would say proudly and show me a new clock or radio, a new vase or a wind-up music box. "You talked about that crazy record with foreigners laughing; you know, the one where you and your friends shrieked with laughter at their strange voices. I finally found a new phonograph with improved sound. Listen to this."

Father's passion for shopping continued unabated. Once when he and I were in a tea garden where tea accessories were sold, he looked at the display of chocolate-colored teapots, each with a different shape. One set was shaped like peaches, another pumpkins, and another the shape of small animals. "I'll take them all," he said, with a wide sweeping gesture to the clerk. Although I enjoyed seeing the tea sets in the house, they gradually disappeared. I believe the servants liked them too.

On one of my weekends at home, I wandered into the guestroom and found the bed made up with new hand-embroidered comforters and pillowcases. Puzzled, I peeked into the chiffonier and discovered delicate handkerchiefs and candies in the top drawer and soft silk underclothes and subtly colored gowns in other drawers.

"What's going on?" I asked Auntie Yuk Ching, who had entered the room behind me.

"You're going to have a new Auntie."

My body went stiff. Who was taking my mother's place? "How did this happen without my knowing?"

"You've been thinking only of school and friends. Your father has had a busy social life."

"You are the matchmaker?"

"Not really." She smiled, and I knew she'd had a hand in the affair. "At a party he spotted a lovely shy eighteen year old girl whose quiet manner and innocent look he liked. Naturally I and his male friends urged him to marry Pun Yun."

"She'll be First wife?"

"No. Second wife. Your father can later marry a First wife if he so desires. Grandma Zee has made all the arrangements."

Following father's and Pun Yun's traditional marriage ceremony, they greeted their guests in our ceremonial hall. It was decorated with garlands of flowers and bright colored material covering the chairs and tables. Slim and beautiful in an embroidered top and long skirt, Pun Yun showed her respect to my mother by kowtowing to her and her ancestors' spirit seats. Doing so, she recognized her place in the family. Then, as Pun Yun sat in the living room, father introduced her to our family and friends. I bowed to her, and as was the custom, she acknowledged me by handing me a gift—a jade green bracelet carved with flowers interspersed with Chinese characters symbolizing beauty.

Guests teased the new couple. In the tradition called *nao sin fon*, they called out to the couple, "We'll only leave you alone, if you reward us." The point was to embarrass the bride and groom. When the guests spotted father's and Pun Yun's discomfort, they howled with laughter and called out rewards that might stop the teasing—"ten boxes of chocolate; 100 yuan."

During the teasing, Sio Ying lingered in the hall outside the living room, her eyes swollen with tears. She might be my father's *Ping-tau*—mistress, but would never be his wife. It would be despicable for a mistress to become a wife, and if she became one, she would not be respected by the family. Chinese customs of family lineage would keep Sio Ying in a secondary position.

I called Pun Yun "Auntie" instead of "mother" and spent pleasant hours talking and going to the movies with her. The cosmopolitan city of Shanghai had many theaters, such as the Nanking Theater, the Grand, and the luxurious Cathay, where tickets cost the equivalent of $1.00. In twenty minutes the rickshaw carried us into town, and we managed to see the two o'clock, five o'clock and the seven o'clock movies before we returned home. Although Pun Yun understood no English, she loved musicals, especially if they featured Nelson Eddy and Jeanette McDonald.

Sio Ying remained the ever-present nemesis to anyone who dared infringe upon her relationship with my father.

"I see you have prepared special marinated strips of thin pork for Lau Ya," Pun Yun said to Sio Ying as they passed each other on the stairs. "That's very thoughtful of you, but you needn't bother. I will see his needs are taken care of now."

"You? You are only Second wife. What standing do you have in this house?"

Although surprised by Sio Ying's frontal attack, Pun Yun still managed to say through stinging tears, "There are special sweet date cakes in the kitchen. I will bring those to him."

"How nice that you bring the cakes that I made," Sio Ying said. "Just like a servant."

Unable to withstand the verbal abuse, Pun Yun ran to her room. What could she do about father's mistress of many years? Nothing. Since she was the Second wife, she had no standing in the family and had to accept the relationship.

However, Pun Yun was not without allies. One night Ah-Bin reported to Auntie Yuk Ching, who was still in charge of the household, that Lau Ya (Big Master) had sent him home alone for the evening.

"So he's staying at that woman's place," she muttered. After a moment's hesitation, she called Auntie Pun Yun to come downstairs. "Ah-Bin," she ordered, "Take Second Tai Tai, U-Ching and Tek Child to Sio Ying's house."

Before we climbed into the car, Auntie whispered careful instructions to Pun Yun about what she should say and do.

A surprised Sio Ying opened her door, but recovered quickly. "How nice of you to visit me at this late hour," she said with sweetness dripping from her small mouth.

Pun Yun stepped forward into the hall and asked, "Is Lau Ya here?"

"Oh, no," replied Sio Ying.

"I apologize for our intrusion," Pun Yun said. "We will leave directly, but may I use the bathroom first?" Not waiting for Sio Ying to answer, she pushed past her and ran toward the staircase. Just as she reached the middle of the stairs, father opened the bedroom door laughing.

Pun Yun stopped and begged. "Please come home with us now." Tears slid down her cheeks.

We returned with Lau Ya that night.

As a youngster I thought the interplay was some kind of an adult game.

Chapter 10

For a time life took on a sameness. Even the drifting toward war between the Japanese, Mao's Communists, and Chiang's Nationalists was only a backdrop for our family's problems.

I continued my studies at Mi Ling School. One day as the chauffeur carried my luggage to the car for my return to school, Auntie Yuk Ching took my hand and led me into the western living room. There U-Ching sat like a small doll on the large sofa. I didn't understand why he was there. We waited impatiently while Auntie doubled over from one of her recent bouts of coughing, which persisted despite her constant use of Chinese herbs.

"I'll be late for school," I complained.

She touched my shoulder, removed her handkerchief from in front of her mouth. "I have something to tell you. I can't wait any longer. U-Ching isn't your real brother, but you have a real sister, and she'll be coming home soon."

"What nonsense!" I thrust my chin forward and glared at her.

"I speak the truth!"

Tek Ying and U-Ching

"Don't be cruel." I pounded my fists on the pillows. "Don't tell me such false things."
"I must tell you."
"I don't want a sister." I shouted and reached for my brother's hand and squeezed it tight. "He's my real brother." Although he didn't understand what was going on, U-Ching began to sob.

U-Ching was only six years old, and I ached for him . . . for us. My world seemed to be falling apart. Although tears spilled down my face, I pulled a piece of candy out of my pocket and popped it into his downturned mouth. He smiled and wiped away his tears.

After I had absorbed the news, I sat dejected next to U-Ching, while Auntie related my mother's story. "Your mother was distressed that she had given birth to a third daughter. She blamed herself. To ease her concern, Auntie Chu took the girl baby to a woman in Wu Sih and brought home a boy baby from the orphanage." Auntie stood very still looking down at me while she explained. "Do you remember when she showed you the baby? You said something like the baby was so white."

"I didn't mean anything by . . ."

"Hush. I'm telling you what happened, not what you want to hear." She put her hand to her mouth as she coughed again. " Do not interrupt. When you commented on the baby's color and size, the aunties realized the baby was too old and not small enough for a newborn, so Auntie Chu returned that baby boy for another. That is how U-Ching came to be your brother."

I sat still, trying to comprehend what she was telling me. "Does father know?"

"I think he always knew, but didn't say anything. When the doctor came out of your mother's room after the birth, he mumbled that Sau Yuk was unhappy about giving birth to another girl. I don't know if Sio Ying overheard. She might have told her suspicions to your father."

"But mother always said how much U-Ching looked like father," I argued.

Auntie Yuk Ching frowned. "That was your mother's way."

"What about the girl baby?" I wanted to know, but I was afraid to hear the answer.

"Your mother never forgot her child. She regularly sent money to the family that raised her. And when she bought something for you, she bought something for her. But after your mother died, no one on her side of the family could afford the expense of taking care of your sister. To solve the problem, the woman who had been taking care of her was going to sell her to a *Tong-Chih* (house of prostitution). If the girl had become a prostitute, your father would have been disgraced. When your mother's brother-in-law found out, he told your father. He settled with the family. Your sister will arrive this week."

I began to understand why the servants and the rest of the family treated U-Ching with indifference. In China the master's concubine and an adopted child are treated in the same manner. Without a firm position in the family, they are shown no respect.

The following weekend I returned home to meet my "new" sister. Father had changed her name to "Sun Mei," "Sun," meaning Shanghai, where she'd been born, and "Mei," for "sister."

I found her character to be disagreeable and her looks unappealing. A skin disease had marked her face. She wore ill-fitting clothes and had poor manners. She came from the peasant world, a world foreign to my upbringing. But while I could go off to school and not be bothered with this "new" sister, the rest of the family united to draw Sun Mei into the ways of the family. Auntie Pun Yun took her to a dermatologist for skin treatments and washed her face daily with special medication. Father ordered bolts of silk and had the tailor make new clothes for Sun Mei. Special candies and boxes of oranges were bought for her, but on my third weekend home, Sun Mei was still tearful, unhappy, a stranger to all of us. We were strangers to her as well. She cried inconsolably for the woman she had known as her mother. But that woman would have sold her to a *Tong-Chih*.

"Stop your incessant crying," Father ordered Sun Mei. But she continued to whine and cry. "Can't you do something with her?" he said to Auntie Yuk Ching.

She bowed, trying to appease my father. "We are trying, brother, but it will take time."

Although U-Ching and Sun Mei were part of our family, throughout their lives, they retained inferior positions in the household. They were sent to local schools, rather than to schools of their choosing. As they did with many family secrets, everybody kept quiet about the entire matter and pretended nothing was odd or different.

Our family was like a dragon with many tails that operated with one head–my father's. But Sio Ying was the neck that turned the head.

Chapter 11

1932

Not until Pun Yun's pregnancy did the household take notice of her. At that moment she became the focus of attention. My aunties fashioned a belt with a piece of white jade hanging so low that it stretched over Pun Yun's belly. Wearing the jade helped insure that she would bear a male child. Father was so concerned about the birth going well that he sent Pun Yun to the hospital several days before the baby was due. With the birth of Shiu Ching, a boy, Pun Yun was moved from her small room to my mother's room and was waited on in every manner to be sure that she and her son would be strong and healthy.

During her first month after the birth, known as the "sitting month," Pun Yun was confined to bed and treated like an invalid. Everything was done to keep her and her son healthy. In order to protect her from catching cold, she was not even allowed to bathe or shampoo her hair. She was not allowed to drink cold water or eat cold fruit or ice cream, since cold items were thought to harm her system. To get rid of the bad blood associated with childbirth, she drank a bitter herb mixture. To replenish her lost blood, she ate constantly.

"I can't eat another bite," Auntie Yun told the maid who brought her chicken soup at midnight.

"You must eat," the maid said. "I keep pork and chicken soups bubbling on the kitchen stove day and night. Lau Ya would be unhappy with me if I didn't see you properly fed."

"I'm beginning to look like a balloon," Auntie Yun said, but took the bowl and began to ladle the thick broth into her mouth.

"Much food gives you much breast milk for your child," her maid said, looking at the baby. "See how big he is. It's a good luck sign when mother and son are fat."

Giving relatives and friends red-dyed boiled eggs announced the birth of Auntie Yun's son. Our family bought hundreds of eggs, which the servants boiled in huge kettles and piled on rattan trays for dyeing. I, along with everyone else, helped in the large kitchen area. I held up my bright red hands, laughing. "Look at my design," I said to my cousin as we bathed the eggs in red dye. With my fingertips, I made red dots into faces on several pre-dyed eggs.

My aunties who bustled about the kitchen made noises like clucking hens. "Cover up the spots," one said.

"We can't deliver dotted eggs," said another.

"I know," I said and immersed the eggs into the red dye pot. I glanced at my cousin and saw she'd also made a design on an egg before she pushed it into the dye vat. We'll all have red hands for days, maybe weeks," I said with delight.

Once the eggs were dried, servants placed them in large baskets and delivered them to close relatives and friends. The closest relative received fifty eggs, and more distant relatives and friends received only ten or twenty.

The birth of a son was and still is very important to a

Chinese family. Even poor families celebrate, especially if the boy is a first born.

Normally after the "sitting month," the next "full month" marks a celebration feast. But because we had so many preparations to make, we held a "double month" feast for my new brother, Shiu Ching, two months after his birth.

The house glowed as if we were celebrating New Year. Wishes for prosperity poured in, in the form of gifts of shimmering giant red silk scrolls decorated with gold paper symbols representing my father's name. Lists of the gift givers covered the entire wall of the Celebration Hall. Candles blazed on the tables set up in the Hall. Each was set for ten guests. Our best embroidered silk covers enhanced the tables as well as the chairs.

Outside, workers set up a straw-plaited canopy covering the entire grounds to protect guests from the intense sun or the possible rains. In the garden a stage for acrobats and singers was constructed just for the evening. Gifts from friends paid for the performances. Close relatives gifted the baby with gold pendants, little golden bells that jingled on his wrist, or lucky paper money folded into red paper.

From the local restaurants, cooks came to our kitchen to prepare the ten different dishes such a celebration feast featured. The cooks spent hours chopping vegetables, meats and seafood. They filled the kitchen with wondrous odors. On each table servants placed four cold dishes of fish, chicken, shrimp, and dipping sauces. When the guests were ready to sit at the tables, they could begin their feast with the cold food. Later, the servants carried in, one by one, steaming platters of the specially prepared foods.

A member of the family at each table served the guests, using chopsticks to refill their bowls as soon as the bowls were empty. If we didn't want more food, we left a small portion in the bowl. Like everyone else I had helpings from each of the hot stir-fry platters—shrimp, chicken diced with vegetables, sea cucumber, abalone and bamboo shoots, sautéed fish. Later the servants brought in whole legs of pork, whole fish and chickens, and ducks stuffed with sweet rice, water lily seeds and dates. Huge ceramic tureens of soup with chicken, mushroom, ham, bamboo shoots and transparent noodles followed. Like a starving peasant, I feasted on everything.

By the time the servants carried in the sweet buns and sweet rice cakes for dessert, I was stuffed. The pace of everyone's chopsticks had slowed. It seemed impossible that anyone could enjoy the morsels of peeled fruit and candies placed on tables throughout the house in gleaming silver and crystal compote bowls.

While others continued eating the desserts, I dropped my chopsticks next to my bowl. My head sagged, and I felt as if my eyes were bulging from all the food I'd consumed. I glanced at one of my Aunties, and she excused me along with several other children. We trudged upstairs, then plopped onto a sofa, groaning from our full bellies. Even the adults required a second day of feasting to finish all the delicacies.

Although I was caught up in the festivities, the birth of my new brother changed my life. One weekend when I came home from school, I walked into a busy house and was ignored. "Where's father?" I asked Auntie Yuk Ching.

"He's with Auntie Yun and the baby." She coughed heavily and began to hurry off.

"Doesn't he know I'm home?" I called after her.

She turned to face me in the hall. "Perhaps. But you must understand . . . he has new duties and responsibilities." She moved to my side and touched my arm. "He might not be so available to you." She glanced at Ah-Bin who waited patiently, holding my luggage. "No need to stand there. Take Tek Child's bags . . . ." She grabbed her chest and crumpled like a doll at my feet.

I reached down to her. "Auntie what's the matter?"

Ah-Bin dropped my bags and lifted her in his arms. "Get Lau Ya!" He laid her on the couch in the living room as I ran to get father.

By the time father arrived, Auntie Yuk Ching was sitting up and drinking tea that one of the servants had brought. "Too much celebrating," she said. But her pale face made me believe she was very sick.

"You must rest." Father ordered a servant to help her to her room.

That weekend and the next four or five were unhappy ones. Auntie stayed in bed, and now I was even more alone. Her words had been prophetic; father was no longer available for me. There were no new gifts from his shopping sprees. Instead he spent his time with Shui Ching and Pun Yun.

As months passed even Ming Li School was not a haven. During the middle of the week, one of my roommate's mothers came to visit her daughter in our dormitory, even though she would see her on the weekend. I watched surreptitiously as mother and daughter sat close together on the girl's bed, whispering and laughing while the mother stroked her daughter's hair. Just as the mother was about to leave, she handed her daughter a bag of chestnuts and told her to share them with her roommates.

Before I returned to school on Monday following my weekend at home, I went to Auntie Yun. "Will you visit me at school this Wednesday?"

She smiled. "But you come home on weekends."

"I know, but it would be nice if you saw how I live at school, in the dorm."

She nodded. "If you wish."

"Oh, and when you come bring seven bags of chestnuts."

Auntie Yun looked puzzled. "Can't you take them from home? Why seven?"

"Please, Auntie, just do this for me." Couldn't she understand that this was important to me?

On Wednesday I peered down the dormitory hall every few minutes in anticipation of her visit. When I saw her coming, I backed into my room and waited for her knock.

I opened the door, she bowed, said "hello," and glanced about the room, and didn't even seem to notice how I had to live at school. "I must go now." She dropped the bag of chestnuts on my bed and left.

I wanted to cry out to her, but instead stood in the doorway and watched her retreating round figure. Half-heartedly I gave each of my roommates a bag of chestnuts and kept two for myself. I ate the chestnuts under my bedcovers late at night while tears splashed upon their crusty sweet meat. For me they had no taste.

Chapter 12

Another year went by, and the clamor of war came closer to Shanghai. On weekends I overheard conversations between father and Yen Tai.

"You mustn't be so down on the Japanese," Yen Tai said. "They are an enlightened people."

"They can stay enlightened in their own country, not mine," father said sharply.

"They will rid China of the Communists. Isn't that your desire?"

Father nodded. "China must be independent of both."

"But you aren't happy with Chiang Kaishek either." Yen Tai tapped his fingertips together in front of his face. "You must choose."

"Must I choose between a yellow dragon, a red dragon and a stripped dragon?" Father's eyes narrowed. "Each has a hot breath that scorches my country."

Was it my imagination or was father now less intrigued with this man I called Uncle Wong? But Yen Tai's wife, Hai Li, smoothed over the small difficulties between my father and her husband and brought happiness to many of us.

Out in the garden she and Grandma Zee discussed Spring Orchid's future while they sat in wooden chairs on the lawn. The Zee girls and I listened. "It's time the girl moved on," Hai Li said. "She's twenty. I've been looking for a new husband for her."

Grandma Zee smiled and nodded. "It's time she established her own family. I will help you. This new husband must be both good and healthy."

"I will enjoy gathering new items for her dowry," Hai Li said, smoothing the edges of her sleeve.

"You will need another maid. I have another *Ya Tua* ready for service," Grandma Zee said.

"No need," said Hai Li. "We may be moving. My husband has business in the north." She looked away from Grandma Zee as if she wanted to end the conversation.

The Zee sisters and I glanced at one another with raised eyebrows, for the only business in the north these days involved the Japanese. None of us reported this conversation to my father, for we knew how he felt about the Japanese.

Despite that inkling of the Wong's impending move, they remained in Shanghai. When Pun Yun gave birth to her second son, Tsu Ching, father asked Yen Tai to become my second brother's godfather. Had Yen Tai's business venture in the north failed to materialize?

While we celebrated Tsu Ching's birth, Auntie Yuk Ching lay dying in her room. All too soon the happiness of a birth was overshadowed by death. Father's youngest sister and manager of the household succumbed to her persistent cough. My cousins and I knelt beside her coffin in the Ceremonial Hall just as I had done after my mother's death. My tears came easily. Never again would her round sweet face be there to comfort me. She had organized and run the household, been a true friend to all the children, but had never married. Her family had been my father's family.

After a few days the coffin was transferred by boat to Wu

Sih, where her relatives attended the funeral. Unlike my mother who had to wait in the Pin Yee Kwon until her husband died before she could be buried, single Auntie Yuk Ching could be buried in the family cemetery right away.

My father had designed the ten acres of cemetery grounds that were enclosed by a brick wall with a huge gate leading into the grounds. Young trees and bushes had been artfully planted so that in later years the area would look like a garden. Brick benches allowed family members to rest, listen to the singing birds and dwell on their memories of those who had gone before.

"She's fortunate," one of my uncles said as we stood in the cemetery garden.

My aunties nodded in agreement. "It was such a beautiful and grand funeral," one said.

"And to be buried next to her parents," another said. "So lucky."

Other relatives bobbed their heads. "Lucky! Very lucky," they agreed.

Lucky? To die of tuberculosis at twenty-five? Poor Auntie Yuk Ching. She had such a limited life. Nothing exciting had ever happened to her. I knew she'd been interested in one of the actors at the local theater, but such a relationship would have been impossible. For her to have married a lower class person would have made my father lose face. She lived and died a single woman.

On a long brick table that ran in front of the graves, we placed bowls of meats and rice and sweet dishes for the spirits of the dead. Then, kneeling in front of the graves, we kowtowed and offered prayers while burning candles, incense, and paper money. Through this ritual we showed our respect toward her and to our other deceased relatives. That day I said my final good-bye to Auntie Yuk Ching

Little did I know how different our life at home would be now that she was gone.

Chapter 13

1935–1937

Once Pun Yun married my father, the intrusive hand of Sio Ying shadowed her life. Auntie Yuk Ching's death intensified that intrusion. By the time Auntie Yuk Ching died, both of Sio Ying's children had married and left home. Now with the last obstacle—Auntie Yuk Ching's death—out of her way, Sio Ying moved into our house as though she were moving into her own home.

The battle was on between Pun Yun and Sio Ying. Ever since their marriage, Father had insisted that Pun Yun account for every penny she spent. But it was not easy for her to write down how she had used the money father gave her, for having grown up in a penniless family, she was illiterate. In China during these years, getting an education was impossible unless the family had money. At first I had helped with writing down the expenses, but after one of my uncles taught Pun Yun to read and write, she managed to do this herself.

One day as Sio Ying, Auntie Yun and I gathered in my

father's room, Auntie Yun said, "I'd like to make a special outfit for Shiu Ching. I will need yuan for material."

Father, who was sitting at his desk, turned to Sio Ying. "I need yuan," he said, gesturing toward a cabinet. "Get it for me from the drawer."

While Pun Yun stood humbly by, Sio Ying went to the cabinet, opened the drawer and withdrew the amount of money she thought Pun Yun should have. This she handed to father who in turn gave it to Pun Yun. "I wish to speak to you about our oldest son," father said to Pun Yun. "You have too much to do, caring for two sons. Sio Ying will care for Shiu Ching from now on."

My hand flew to my mouth. Pun Yun stood motionless, her hand that held the yuan trembled. She stared at father, but refused to look at the smirking Sio Ying.

"It's no trouble to take care of our two sons. They are good children and make little work. I take great pleasure in taking care of them."

"We both love our sons. Sio Ying loves him too. She will be in charge of him whenever his nanny is otherwise occupied."

Sio Ying looked up from her chair with a smirk on her face. "Don't worry," she said to Pun Yun. "I will have him sleep in my room and treat him like my own son. Now you won't need the money after all, for I will order him a special outfit."

Father rose. "Sio Ying, your whole-hearted acceptance of Shiu Ching delights me."

Pun Yun handed the yuan to father, bowed and left the room. Her shoulders sagged. I started to cry out at the injustice of his dictate, but father turned toward me with a stern frown. I knew that look and followed Auntie out of the room. What could I do? I knew father's ploy wouldn't make Sio Ying any more acceptable to the family, although that's probably what he had in mind.

When Shiu Ching started to talk, he was taught to call Sio Ying, *Mmei*,—mother in Soochow dialect. In our Shanghai dialect, we called our mothers *Mma*. Shui Ching called his real mother, Pun Yun, *Mma*.

During meals at the large formal table, Pun Yun sat at one end of the table and my father at the other end with the rest of my aunties and uncles, their older children and father's children in between. Sio Ying's place was directly to father's right, where she sat with downcast eyes. Was she feeling the dislike of the rest of the family? Father remained stoic at meals, despite the obvious tension.

Father turned to me at lunch one afternoon and said, "It would be nice, Tek Child, if you called Sio Ying, "Foreign Mma".

I stared at him. "She's not my *Mma*!"

Only the click of chopsticks and Sio Ying's sniffling broke through the curtain of silence. Sio Ying's body tensed as she stared down at her rice bowl. A twinkle of amusement shown in the eyes of my other aunties and uncles. They would never say anything to father (Lau Ya) directly, but they weren't interested in giving Sio Ying, the sexy demon wolf, any further rights.

Sio Ying sat with tears in her eyes as she moved her chopsticks aimlessly around the food in her bowl, not eating. The meal, like others of late, became uncomfortable. Father rose in the middle of his lunch and left the table without saying a word.

The next day he did not come to the table at mealtime. My aunties, afraid for his health, whispered amongst themselves. "We can't let Lau Ya go without food." Auntie Yun, unable to do anything else, ordered the cook to take Lau Ya's meal to Sio Ying's room. Father never ate at the table with us again. He, Sio Ying and my brother, Shiu Ching, took meals together in Sio Ying's room. Neither I nor anyone else dared say anything.

Not content with her victory with Shui Ching, Sio Ying moved my father's clothes into several armoires in her room and personally played to father's fastidious behavior. Once he had worn an article of clothing, she, not a maid, would either wash and press or brush it before returning it to the armoire. On the days when he left the house to engage in business, he wore a westernized suit, shirt and tie instead of his traditional Chinese gown. Sio Ying, not Pun Yun, made sure the right attire was ready for him.

Wu Pei Ching, Tek Ying's Father

Even in summertime he always looked elegant, dressed all in white. First he put on silk undergarments. Over that he wore a long-sleeved Chinese silk tunic and pants covered by a long hand-woven linen gown. His shoes were white canvas, and a white straw hat sat smartly on his head.

At twenty Auntie Yun was young and pretty, but her husband was controlled by a forty-year-old woman who was two years older than my father. Pun Yun began to fuel her frustration with food, eating sweets and gorging herself on bean curd pastries. During this time she was still nursing her new son, Tsu Ching, and she grew fatter and fatter.

Dark clouds followed Sio Ying into our house, angering the Kitchen god. Sio Ying's actions complicated the intrigue at home.

Third Auntie Yuk Ying, another of father's younger sisters, her daughter and her husband were living a frugal existence in Wu Sih. My father, who felt close to this sister, decided to improve her living conditions. He bought a hardware store in Hangchow, two and a half hours from Shanghai by train, and hired Third Auntie's mild-mannered husband to manage the store. Father offered the hospitality of our house to this sister so that the couple could save money. She and her young daughter moved in with us. Her husband would only be able to visit her once a month in Shanghai, but this didn't seem to bother Third Auntie.

I, together with the other children in the house, delighted in visiting Third Auntie's spacious accommodations in the back part of our house near the household rice storage room. After school my cousins scampered upstairs to Third Auntie's room to laugh, play and enjoy special snacks. The children behaved for her because she told them stories and introduced exciting new games.

"It isn't right that the children gather in the back part of the house with the servants," father said, during a discussion in his office with Auntie Yuk Ying and two of my other aunties.

"But they have so much fun," one of my aunties said. "It keeps them from getting into other mischief."

"I enjoy the children, big brother," Auntie Yuk Ying said. "Please let me do this small thing in return for your hospitality."

"You've added to Ah-Bin's duties as chauffeur." Father looked out the window as if he were intent on the garden. "You ask him to bring back special treats of honey rice cakes. Once he brought baked ground pork dumplings."

"We asked him to do that, not Third Auntie," one of the other aunties said.

"He brings the treats to my room for the children," Auntie Yuk Ying said.

"I know they're for the children." He turned and looked at all the women in front of him. "You all approve of this arrangement?"

They nodded with smiles upon their faces. Father relented and allowed his household to continue to bubble with these activities.

On weekends I joined Auntie Yuk Ying's happy group and enjoyed the treats that Ah-Bin brought. Like a shadow he came and went, doing the same job he'd done for eighteen years. He was divorced, sensitive and patient, with an angular acerbic face that reflected strength.

One day while my maid was cleaning my room, she whispered to me. "Something ugly is happening. The other servants gossip about an affair."

"I don't want to hear your gossip," I said, but I knew the house was rife with rumors. Despite my reluctance to learn anything bad about Third Auntie, the following weekend I couldn't help listening to my maid's breathless tale.

"Cook went up to the rice room early in the morning and found Ah-Bin in your Third Auntie's room." My maid was shaking as she rattled off the tale to me. "Naturally cook was outraged. She tattled to Sio Ying."

I said nothing to my maid, but I knew Sio Ying had been looking for a way to regain what stature she had in the household. Would this incident give her that chance?

A frightening event had happened just the weekend before. Sio Ying's son, Gun Yuen, had stormed into the house and threatened father with a gun. "I'll not have my mother living in your house as a mistress," he shouted. His body quivered with rage, and the pistol shook in his hand. "I'm called a turtle, allowing my mother to be dishonored."

Father strode forward and faced his angry red-faced son. "Your mother has no dishonor in this house. It's you who cause disgrace by storming in here with unacceptable words."

Gun Yuen yelled into father's face as he jabbed the gun into father's stomach. "You've never honored my mother."

Father glanced at the gun, then stared into Gun Yuen's eyes. "I am your father. Are you going to kill your own father?" No one moved. Tension rose like steam. Finally, father broke the silence. "We can't change the past or even the future."

"Everyone knows you're my father, but you refuse to honor me as a son! Yang was more father to me than you."

"You know as well as I do that you can't call me 'father' in public. That's why you call me 'cousin.' Does it make the truth less a truth?"

Gun Yuen's eyes glinted as he continued to menace father with the gun. Father didn't retreat, but he didn't reach for the gun either. Sio Ying hurried to her son's side. "You are not to say such things," she said with her face close to Gun Yuen's. "I'm here of my own accord. Do not meddle where you understand little. Wu Pei Ching has provided you with your education, your car, all of your needs. He has tried to take full responsibility for you as a father. Does that have no meaning to you?"

The trio stood statue like as the antique clock ticked on through the tense silence. Finally, Gun Yuen lowered the gun and stepped back, his handsome face distorted with rage.

"Someday ... someday, the turtle will turn into a dragon." He turned his back on father and Sio Ying and marched out of the house with the gun still clutched in his hand.

The gun incident might have shaken Sio Ying's confidence in her place in the house if Third Auntie hadn't been living with us. But the news about Third Auntie gave Sio Ying a chance to turn father's attention to a different scandal.

"Sio Ying hammer on your father day and night," my maid said. "Third Auntie evil, she told him. Third Auntie bring disfavor to Wu house. Third Auntie should not stay in Wu house. On and on she go after your poor Third Auntie."

"But Third Auntie is still here," I said, trying to quiet her hysterical talk.

She shook her head. "Master fire Ah-Bin."

Months later Third Auntie had a new baby boy. Soon after on a Saturday afternoon, walking by my father's study, I heard weeping and peered into the room. Father sat at his desk, staring at a stack of papers before him. Third Auntie stood in front of him, crying and holding her new baby son in her arms. Without looking up from his desk, father said, "If you leave this house, you'll never come back."

Third Auntie did leave. She settled into a small apartment with Ah-Bin. Months later a cousin and I visited her. She seemed quite happy with her two children, despite the fact that her husband had divorced her and my father had disowned her. Although we didn't see Ah-Bin, we learned that among their circle of friends they were man and wife.

When I returned from my visit to Third Auntie's, I knocked on father's bedroom door, the one that joined my room to his, and entered. He was lounging in a chair reading a newspaper. He smiled at me, but I was in no mood for pleasant talk.

"I've just come from visiting Third Auntie," I announced.

He threw the newspaper aside and glared at me. "Why have you done this? You know she has brought scandal to this house, to me, to the family. Her name will never again be mentioned in this house by you or by any of our relatives."

I vented my indignation at him. "How can you act that way toward her? She's your own sister. You're just a snob!"

Never had I talked to him that way. His eyes and mouth opened wide in astonishment. I turned on my heels and fled from his room into mine, slamming the door behind me. This was the first of our serious disagreements, but the worst was yet to come.

Chapter 14

One afternoon Auntie Yun ran into father's room where Sio Ying sat sewing and talking to father. Auntie waved a photograph of herself that usually stood on her dresser next to a picture of my father. "Look what she did," Pun Yun screamed, pointing to the picture she waved in front of father's face. "She's devil-minded. She has no right to ruin my picture." Pun Yun held up the photo of herself. Where her eyes had been there were now two pinholes. Auntie Yun cried loud and hard as if she herself had been blinded. There could be only one culprit for such a deed.

Sio Ying tittered and turned her head away.

Pun Yun screamed at Sio Ying, "You don't deserve to live in this house."

"I live here. I belong here," Sio Ying shouted back at her.

Pun Yun paused, pulled back her shoulders and raised her chin. She pointed a curved first finger toward herself and said, "I was the woman Lau Ya carried in his car to this house, and we held a ceremony honoring me as his wife."

Sio Ying flung aside her sewing. She whimpered to father. "Pun Yun insults me." When father remained silent, she said again, "I belong here. Why don't you give a party to honor me?"

Father sighed, shook his head, and quietly said, "Only in the next life."

The jealousy between Sio Ying and Pun Yun spilled over into all our social functions, creating a special problem for father when he entertained guests. He wouldn't ask either woman to be hostess; besides it wasn't appropriate to ask a mistress to be hostess. Instead, to avoid creating a scene between Pun Yun and Sio Ying, he asked me to play that role. At home from high school on weekends, I dressed up in lovely cheongsams and played hostess for father.

On one special occasion both Sio Ying and Pun Yun stayed upstairs, while I performed my duties of greeting the guests, bowing and listening to their boring adult conversations. Sio Ying settled herself by the upstairs rail. From there she could peek down without being seen to witness the arrival of the guests. After dinner, when father's guests had settled down to play mah-jongg and poker, I excused myself and went upstairs.

Sio Ying had gone to her room. "Tek Child, come here!" she hissed at me. I lingered at the landing of the second floor, refusing to go to her.

"Tek Child, please come in. I'd like to talk to you."

I shrugged and remained where I was. She came out of her room and tugged at my arm. "Come into my room. What did you think of the ladies' dresses?" When I didn't respond, she continued. "I'm thinking of cutting my hair and having a perm like those ladies. What did you think of Mrs. Chang's green silk dress? Didn't it have a bamboo spray of velvet down the front?"

I shrugged. "I didn't pay much attention." To myself I mused that the ladies downstairs didn't have half-bound feet and were much younger than Sio Ying.

"Did they like the meal? What did they talk about?"

"I did my duties as father wanted me to," I said in a bored voice. "Their talk is of no interest to me." Before continuing on down the hall, I said, "I'm glad my duties are finished for the night. I'm tired and I want to go to bed." I smiled to myself. Sio Ying's unfulfilled desire to be the hostess, to be at father's side, to greet special people obsessed her. Father's answer to her wishes was always, "not in this life." This made me feel good.

Sio Ying's devious behavior had surfaced earlier in the year when she'd asked me to take her to the same tailor Pun Yun had visited. "I need to have an otter collar for my wool coat. The tailor that Pun Yun used was excellent. Won't you take me there?"

Reluctantly, I went with her and directed our new chauffeur to the famous tailor's store. Once we were inside, the tailor welcomed me as Miss Wu, then turned to serve Sio Ying. "Mrs. Wu, what can I do for you?"

I kept quiet. As he continued to call Sio Ying, "Mrs. Wu," she preened and carried on in a grand manner, for this title gave her momentary satisfaction. I watched her in silence, kneading the inside of my pockets. That's what she wants, all right. She's always wanted to be Mrs. Wu. Inwardly I smiled, knowing that this would never happen.

I should have known that Sio Ying's desire to be the main woman in father's life would affect all her actions. But during one happy occasion, I let my guard down. My father had played the role of matchmaker for one of his friend's sons. After the wedding it's the custom for the bridegroom's family to send presents to the matchmaker and his wife. While father, Auntie Yun and Sio Ying sat in the main room watching, I eagerly opened the brightly wrapped gifts. One by one I undid the paper on the gifts to find cakes, candies, ham, ginseng, brandy, and other special treats. One gift was especially for Mrs. Matchmaker—a beautiful piece of brown silk brocaded material.

This gift presented my father with a dilemma. Auntie Yun, as his second wife, was entitled to receive the lovely material. But father knew that if he gave it to her, Sio Ying would be furious, even though she was only his mistress, with no position in the family. Yet he couldn't give it to Sio Ying. He hesitated when I held up the material, thought a moment, and said, "Tek Child, you keep it."

"Father, how wonderful." For a moment I thought of poor Auntie Yun, but I knew she'd never been a fighter for her rights. She wouldn't ask for the gift. It was best that it go to me.

Laying the silk aside, I turned to unwrap the next gift. As I did so, Sio Ying picked up the material, smiled sweetly and said, "I'll keep it for you until you're ready to use it. All right?" I agreed, thinking that I could retrieve the material from Sio Ying whenever I wanted to have a dress made for a special occasion.

Chapter 15

While the tension with Sio Ying continued at home, other outside activities took over my thoughts, especially the situation growing out of the phone call from my friend, Illan. At Ming Li High School my beautiful, imaginative, and talented sixteen-year-old schoolmate, Illan, had taken me into her confidence. She was two years older than I. She painted, carved lovely works in soapstone, knitted like a professional and wrote poetry. As if that weren't enough, she dressed exquisitely. I thought she had the poise and beauty of the American movie star, Norma Shearer. Needless to say, I was her admirer, as well as her friend.

Illan's family was even more old-fashioned than mine. Her father, a well-to-do businessman, ruled the house and made the decisions. As was often the case in such families, Illan's father kept two concubines. Her mother remained a traditional, obedient first wife; her sisters and brother had married and had produced the expected children.

Intelligent and rebellious Illan was an alien in this traditional family structure. She was filled with new ideas, perhaps a foreshadowing of her doom.

"I've got someone I want you to meet," she told me over the phone. "Sidney Chao. He's twenty-four, he's studied in America and is a graduate of St. John's University in Shanghai. He works for a foreign firm here in Shanghai."

"Father would never let me see anyone alone on a social basis." I said.

"Don't tell him. I'm certainly not going to tell my father. Next Sunday we'll go have tea at Sidney's apartment."

"What about your fiancée?"

Illan made a face. "You know how I feel about my arranged marriage."

"But he's from such a wealthy and well-known Shanghai family. Your family is making elaborate preparations for your wedding."

"Will you forget my coming marriage. It's time-consuming enough. I want to have fun before I have to settle down. I can't be seen alone with Sidney, and I know you'll like him."

"Shall we include Lucy?"

"Lucy would only tell everyone. She's too conservative, too . . . well, you know."

I finally agreed, and on my next weekend at home Illan and I went to visit Sidney at his large apartment. A clean-cut young man dressed in a western business suit opened the door to our ring and welcomed us with a smile. I was thrilled at this adventure of being with sixteen-year-old Illan and an older man. In Sidney's modern-styled living room, maids served tea and imported biscuits.

"Sidney enjoys films," Illan said, trying to start the conversation.

"I prefer American films," Sidney said. "After you've been to America, you find Chinese films very unconvincing."

Naturally Sidney would like American films. Chinese spoke of those who had studied in America as having been dipped in gold.

"There are some newer Chinese films, like 'Queen of Sports,' that are quite good," Illan said.

I'd seen that with Auntie Yun, but I remained quiet as the two talked about many things I didn't fully grasp.

"Sidney, are you in the movie business?" I finally asked.

Sidney threw back his head and laughed. "I wish I were. No. I work in an import export firm with headquarters in London."

Illan and Sidney continued to talk about the American cinema, while I tried to keep up with the discussion. At the end of the tea when Illan and I had to leave, Sidney asked, "When can we meet again?"

Illan and I looked at each other, for we knew we were wrong conducting a secret "rendezvous." Nevertheless, we made an elaborate plan for our next meetings. Illan would call me at a specific time, and I would stay by the phone to insure that no one else in the family answered the ring. At her call we would specify the place, day and time of our next meeting.

Our first outing was at the Cathay Theater, where Charlie Chaplin's movie, "Modern Times," was playing. As planned, Sidney arrived first at the theater and bought the tickets. Sober-faced, he slipped me the tickets as Illan and I sauntered past. We stood apart from him until the lobby lights lowered and the auditorium darkened; then we all hurried in and eased ourselves into our seats. Illan sat in the middle, saying it wouldn't look right for Sidney to sit between us. I was enthralled with Chaplin's comic dance to the tune of "T. Tina, Mine Tina." But then I noticed the two of them holding hands and felt apprehensive. Still, the intrigue was exciting, and I refused to acknowledge that Illan was using me to allow her to see Sidney without causing a scandal.

As Illan's wedding plans became more involved, she was forced to withdraw from school. She continued her studies at home. I would meet her on weekends, either at my home or at one of our "rendezvous" with Sidney. Gradually, Illan had more and more difficulty getting out of the house. In the beginning we had met once a week; then it stretched to once a month. Eventually, neither Sidney nor I heard from her, and we concluded that she had gotten caught up in preparations for her marriage. But when I came home one weekend, I saw a letter posted from Peking lying on my small rosewood desk in my room. Puzzled, I tore it open and began reading.

"I hope you will not be as shocked as my parents were to hear that I broke my engagement and have run away from home with Ben Chou, my sister's husband."

The letter nearly slipped from my fingers. I sat down abruptly. What had she done? Through misty eyes, I read on.

"I'm studying art at Peking Art College. Ben and I are very much in love. I could not bear to be smothered by my family. Do not forget me. I'm happy and content. I look forward to a bright and happy future."

I thought of my beautiful and willful friend. How could she have done such a thing? She'd not only ruined her reputation, but she'd humiliated her father and betrayed her sister.

Although I'd known that I'd been used to shield Illan's good name from gossip, I had not understood that her only interest in Sidney came from her desire to get out of the house and away from the duties of her pending marriage. How would Sidney feel about the deception?

Soon after I received the letter, Illan's distraught mother came to my dormitory room. When I opened the door, she rushed in with tears running down her face. Before I could say anything, she tugged at my sleeve. "My daughter's missing. Please. I beg you tell me where my daughter has gone!"

"I don't know," I stammered and pulled away from her. But she cornered me between my bed and the window.

"Please. You were her best friend, her only friend. You were always together. You must know where she went. I beg of you as a filial daughter to your father, you cannot withhold such information."

I couldn't bring myself to tell the truth. "I . . . I'm sorry, but I really don't know. I haven't seen her in months."

"Our family has been dishonored. Does this have no meaning to you? I must know where she went." She clasped her hands to her heart.

"I would tell you if I knew," I lied.

Illan's sobbing mother turned to leave then looked back at me. Guilt swept over me. After she left, I sank onto my bed, for my knees wouldn't stop shaking.

Months went by and the gossip about Illan died down. Sidney and I sort-of dated, going to a movie occasionally. However, our "dates" ended up with our talking about Illan, going over and over what could have been and what had happened instead. I never allowed him to see me home, fearing my father would find out about my meetings. Sidney would call me a cab or a rickshaw and arrange to get in touch with me later.

While I was busy with my social life, my father's and Yen Tai's arguments about their business partnership and the involvement of father's family increased. One day I overheard them as they sat in our garden and I peeked out the window.

"Your cousins took a loan from our bank," Yen Tai said. "Now they live lavishly. Instead of eating at home with their families, they dine at restaurants, frequent shows, gamble, and entertain women. They have squandered the loan!"

"I'll speak with them." Father folded his arms across his chest.

"Too late. They invested in the stock market. A man came to see me yesterday and expected me as co-owner of the bank to pay their gambling debt. Me! Must we protect our collateral by paying off their debts? I didn't bargain for this type of activity. The bank will lose money. I want out of our partnership."

Father sighed. With his belief that his cousins' debts

were his because cousins were family, what options did he have? He bought Yen Tai's share of the bank and to prevent his cousins from going to prison, father paid their debts as well. He closed the rice store in his Li building and later leased the same space to another man who reopened the store. It was again a successful enterprise. Father could only shake his head. Eventually he sold the bank—one of his few unsuccessful ventures.

Soon after this incident, I came home on a weekend to learn the Wongs had left the apartment without warning. Auntie Yun told me father had secluded himself in his office. When I entered after knocking, I found father sitting in his favorite chair staring at the wall.

"I heard the Wongs have left," I said.

He nodded without turning around.

"Did he say good-bye?"

"It's of no consequence. He's gone. North, I think. Peking." He refused to face me.

"Oh, why would he do that?" I questioned.

His voice, usually so forceful, quivered. "He's joined the Japanese."

All I could say was, "I'm sorry, father."

He cleared his throat. "The yellow dragon has swallowed a good man. He would not have gone if they hadn't offered him a powerful position."

I didn't know how to give father sympathy. And would he have accepted it?

"We will not talk of him further." He rose, walked to the window, opened it and breathed deeply.

There was pain inside father. I knew that ever since Zhang Zoulin's assassination by the Japanese, father would have nothing to do with them.

Were we all destined to have our hearts broken by "trusted friends?"

Chapter 16

1936–1938

During this period when my country thrashed through war and rebellion, I continued with my studies and began to prepare to enter a university. While I was studying for entrance exams, I received a letter from Illan. Almost a year had passed since she'd left for Peking. The letter was brief. "I'm back in Shanghai, staying at my sister's house. Please visit me at her house as soon as you can."

I stared at the name and address. This was the same sister whose husband Illan had run off with. That same day I went to her. When I arrived at the house, I was shown into a back room. Illan came forward to greet me. We clasped each other's hands and wept.

"Thank you for coming, my dear friend. I've had one foot in the grave, but I lived."

Immediately I knew she'd had a child. In China the expression, "one foot in the grave," was used to speak of childbirth because of the death rate of mothers.

"Come and see my baby girl." She pulled me forward.

Too shocked to speak, I followed her as she led me to a basket that held a miniature Illan, a beautiful baby girl.

"Isn't she lovely. Mother says I must give her up so I can start life anew. I don't want to, but I have little choice. Mother's enrolled me in evening business English classes. I need to get a job."

I sat down on the mat next to the baby's basket and Illan. "You aren't with Ben any more?"

She shook her head. "I'm hiding from Ben. I fear what he may do now that I've left him." She paused, taking note of my surprised expression. "My sister has forgiven me."

"I'm glad your family is standing by you."

She stared at her baby. "Father has disowned me."

Knowing how old-fashioned her family was, I wasn't too shocked at this news, but my heart hurt for her. "Have you contacted Sidney?"

She picked up her baby. "Sidney is not part of my life now. But you may tell him about me."

Illan and I talked awhile and I cooed over her baby, but it was not like old times between us. When I left her, I felt a strange premonition. Beautiful and talented Illan now faced a bitter life.

Two months later, she called and asked me to meet her in a nearby park. It was a cold winter day, and her face was muffled in a scarf. When she turned to greet me, I was aghast to see her beautiful face sallow and sad. What else could have happened?

"I'm desolate, Tek. The couple I gave my baby to are opium addicts. I visit and see how they smoke around her. What will they do with my child? They might use her for bad purposes when she's older."

There was little I could say to calm her fear. The outlook for her child was dim, and I could offer few words of comfort.

A week after meeting with Illan, I received a call from

Sidney. From the way he said my name, I knew something was wrong. I sank into the black walnut desk chair in our study. "Have you read the paper?" Sidney asked. "She's dead! Our beautiful Illan is dead!" I could hear his tears through the crackling phone line.

I couldn't respond. The phone was a dead weight in my hand, and I stared at the wall with unseeing eyes. We both were silent, unable to communicate our grief.

After a moment he continued, giving me the news in halting sentences. "Ben Chou came to take Illan back to Peking with him. She refused. He stabbed her, then gave himself up to the police. They have him now."

"She was only seventeen, just two years older than I," I said, thinking out loud. Sidney's voice came over the line interrupting my thoughts. "She could have refused to marry a man she didn't love without destroying her whole life. She should have known what kind of man Ben was. Only an irresponsible man would leave his wife and children."

I hung up on Sidney and in a trance moved upstairs to my room. Of course, Sidney was right; Illan's headstrong behavior had shaped her destiny. Through tears I looked up at Illan's painting that hung on my bedroom wall. She had painted orchids, the delicate flower the name "Illan" stands for. I cried myself to sleep.

Over a period of time, Sidney and I saw one another on a weekly basis, dropping into a coffeehouse for tea after a movie. Other times we sought out a ballroom for afternoon tea dancing. Our dates always ended before dark; I considered myself a nice, decent girl and knew I shouldn't be out with a man after dark. Our main topic of conversation no matter what we did was Illan.

For Sidney's birthday I made round pillows of black, gold, and yellow silk satin. The black material formed the base for a gold and yellow sunflower I sewed in the center. I surprised myself at how well they turned out. I gave him the present when I went to his apartment for a party he was having. He was delighted with my gift, which made me proud. The pillows were my first handiwork worthy of a tribute.

After the other guests left, Sidney and I sat in front of the fireplace, his arm around my shoulders and our heads pressed together.

"It was a nice party," I said. "Your friends are . . . "

"Nice. Sometimes I go crazy with nice," he said. "Maybe that's what happened to Illan. She wanted more from life."

"We all want more. I'm just not sure what exactly I do want. Father wants me to go to the university. I must honor his wish."

"Of course, you should."

We continued to sit side by side on the sofa. I could hear his soft breathing and smell his aftershave. I thought of my father's 4711 cologne. Suddenly Sidney brushed his cheek against mine, and before I knew it, his lips touched mine.

Surprised at the pleasurable feeling his kiss elicited, I pulled away, jumped to my feet and grabbed my coat. Sidney stood next to me with an anxious look on his face.

"Ah Tek what're you doing? There's nothing to get upset about."

"I'm not upset. I have to leave, that's all." I dashed out the door with Sidney at my heels.

"Wait. Wait. You mustn't be upset. Will I see you tomorrow?"

I waved at a passing rickshaw and scrambled inside. Sidney ran after me, trying to talk to me as the rickshaw man pulled away.

I mumbled with my head bowed, "I'll call you." The rickshaw spun down the road, leaving Sidney standing in the street, while I felt my hot cheeks and fought back confused thoughts.

At home that night I sat at the table with the family, but I couldn't eat. Finally, I excused myself and went up to bed.

But sleep wouldn't come. All night I tossed and turned. Every time I closed my eyes, I felt his lips lingering on mine. I liked the feeling, but was confused because I felt I'd done something wrong. But how could something so pleasurable be wrong?

As we had planned at the birthday tea, we met the next day at the Nanking Theater. I watched him walking up to me and was surprised to see he had brought along a boyfriend. Was he trying to soothe my old-fashioned fears? Kissing a boy seemed like a serious commitment; if you kissed a boy, you meant to marry him. Sidney was twenty-six and I just sixteen, with years of school ahead of me. I wasn't ready to think of marriage.

After the evening at the Nanking Theater, I seldom heard from Sidney. Later I met a friend of his who said that Sidney was to be married. Would I ever meet him again? Perhaps it was best we had gone our separate ways. I finished my studies and hoped to enter the University of Soochow, not knowing that cataclysmic events would change my plans.

Chapter 17

Since father had been deprived of a formal education, he was determined that all five of his children graduate from the university. Because I was the first child, it was up to me to set the example. Upon father's insistence, I took the entrance exam to Soochow University and to my amazement passed the test. Although it was unusual for a girl to go to a university outside of her own city, I accepted the opportunity with the same naiveté that had drawn me into the intrigue with Illan and Sidney.

    I boarded the train with father for the 195 kilometer trip to Soochow to begin my entry into university life. The express train sped along, past water buffalo grazing in the green fields, where small wooden farmers' huts huddled together. Young naked children stopped their play in the fields, stood with their fingers in their mouths and watched as our train hurtled past. When the train pulled into Soochow, a flutter played in my stomach, and I twisted the handle of my purse back and forth.

    When father walked forward to choose our rickshaws from the long line of waiting coolies, I hung back. Could I manage this new life away from home? With reluctance I climbed into the rickshaw behind father's. We left the train station behind and soon entered through the university gates and toured the campus grounds. Father pointed to the different buildings, orienting me as well as himself. "The campus is quite small, yet it has all the facilities of a larger university. It should be easy for you to find your way around."

Since registration didn't take place until the following day, he suggested we have a nice dinner. After checking into the fine Garden Hotel, we dined at a famous restaurant, the *Soon Ngo Lau*, "The Chamber of Pine and Flamingo."

When the waiter came to our table, father ordered a special dish called "Three-Shrimp-Over-The-Bridge noodles." "I know how you love shrimp," he said to me with a twinkle in his eyes.

"Very special delicacy," the waiter said. "This dish is served only during the season the shrimp form eggs. Would you like to have fresh river fish and baby leaves of snow peas afterward?"

"Wonderful," father said, agreeing to this delicacy as well.

During the meal, I picked at my food.

"Don't you like it?" father asked, staring at my bowl.

"It's delicious." I put another morsel into my mouth.

He watched me for a moment, then said, "You will do well at school."

I smiled and moved the shrimp around my bowl, unable to force down another bite.

"Remember to be a tiger just like you are at home."

"Yes. I will." I looked at father's unfinished bowl. "Don't you like the snow peas?"

He pushed his bowl away and laid down his chopsticks. "I find I'm not too hungry after all."

We left the restaurant with the waiter shaking his head at his two customers who ordered much and ate little.

Early the next morning before leaving the hotel to travel

the forty minutes to the university by rickshaw, I knocked on father's door. He came to the door in his pajamas. We stared at each other, trying to read each other's eyes.

"Good-bye, father." I bowed and hesitated.

"Be sure to call me," he said.

I nodded and walked down the hall, then turned to wave. He was dabbing at his eyes with a white handkerchief. Outside, as my tears mixed with the lightly falling rain, I climbed into the covered rickshaw. It swayed as it trundled me off toward the university.

When the rickshaw man stopped in front of the main university building, I hastily wiped my eyes. I had cried all the way. The man unhooked the oily cover to let me out. His cotton shirt was soaked through, his hair plastered against his weathered face, and cold misery showed in the set of his jaw. I felt as miserable as he looked and gave him a few extra coins to appease my own unhappiness.

I alighted from the rickshaw, took a deep breath and headed through the university gate toward an office building. There I joined a long line of waiting students. When I reached the office window, I found I was standing in the wrong line. A senior student noticed my confusion and pointed to the correct building. I wandered from building to building and room to room, filling out forms and claiming past college credits due me from advanced studies. Totally depressed with the overwhelming task at hand, I found a phone and rang father at his hotel.

"Are you all right?" he asked.

"Yes," I answered in a choked voice.

"Take care of yourself," he said. "If you need anything, write, but in any case, write once a week. I'll take the next train back home. All right?"

"Yes."

"Good-bye for now . . . tiger."

That did it. I hung up, burst into tears and stumbled

away from the phone while students standing nearby gaped at my behavior.

The first day of classes was a blur. I arrived late for one class, completely missed another, and by the time I reached my dorm room and fell into bed, I couldn't remember whether I'd even had lunch or dinner.

One of my three roommates, surprised by my emotional reaction, said, "You aren't the only frightened one."

The two others laughed and pointed at the room opposite ours. "There's another, 'crying baby,' in there. Come on, snap out of it. There's much to do and see. There's no time for such foolishness." When I couldn't be consoled, they grabbed my hands, pulled me across the hall, opened the door to the other room and pushed me in. "Now you two can cry together," they said and left me with a petite young woman whose western name was Maria. The two of us did cry together—for days. Eventually, Maria and I became best friends, and even now, years and years later we laugh about being the "crying babies."

* * *

I lasted two months at the university before returning home to visit. Ah Gan, our chauffeur, was to meet me at the train in Shanghai. When I spotted him among the crowd, I waved my arms over my head and ran to him calling, "Hello, hello."

For a moment he only stared at me. What could be the matter? Finally he stammered, "Oh, I'm sorry. I didn't recognize you. You've changed."

Indeed I had. In those two months I had gained twenty pounds. At the breakfasts served at the university, I lavishly spread butter on the large, sweet steamed roll and ate it with relish. My "study" habits included hurrying into town with classmates after classes to buy pine nuts, spiced watermelon seeds and candies. At night while I half-heartedly did my homework, I nibbled on these tidbits. I spent more time dipping my greedy hands into the sweets than I did reading and writing.

Now that I was home, I thought about the coming new year, and my thoughts returned to the "matchmaker gift" of silk material that Sio Ying said she would keep for me. I decided I would have a new quilted dress made of my beautiful brocade material. I trotted off to Sio Ying's room.

"I'm ready to use the material you've been keeping for me," I said.

Her eyes narrowed. "What material?"

"Don't you remember?" I said. "The present for Mrs. Matchmaker that father said I should have."

"Ooh? "The present was for Mrs. Matchmaker," Sio Ying said. "Are you Mrs. Matchmaker?"

"Just who are you?" I said. "Are you Mrs. Matchmaker? You're nobody in this house."

Sio Ying sat like a stone statute.

My face got hot, and I clenched my hands. "Where's the material? It's mine," I screamed.

When she refused to give me the material, I rushed out of her room, ran downstairs to the kitchen, grabbed an empty beer bottle, and headed back upstairs. I flung open the door to her room and stormed in, swinging the beer bottle in a large arc. I smashed the mirrors on five armoires. Then with a swipe, I knocked the perfume bottles off her dresser and sent them crashing to the floor. I stood there breathing hard and glared, first at the beer bottle that was now broken and a lethal weapon, then at a terrorized and open-mouthed Sio Ying. "Evil woman! I'll take care of you!" I flung the weapon aside and dashed out the door and downstairs to find another bottle to use as a club.

By the time I got back to her room with another bottle, Sio Ying had locked her door. I spied the open hinged glass window above the door and threw the bottle at it. That done, I spun around and ran into Auntie Yun's room next door. I spotted the specially ordered porcelain teacups and saucers from a round tea table and grabbed them. Auntie Yun, holding out her hands, implored, "Please, please, stop." Instead, I rushed back out into the hall. One by one I flung the precious objects through the open hinged window, hearing them shatter into bits on the other side. A servant scuttled down the stairs to find my father.

Father clamored up the stairs two at a time. "Stop! Stop this right now. You're going to kill someone!"

Through gasps and tears, I shouted, "She won't give me my material!" Father stared at me. Didn't he understand? "I want her out the house. Get her out of here! She's destroying our family."

After a moment of glaring silence, father seized a rosewood stool and slammed it on the hall floor. "I give you everything you need or want. Don't meddle in my private affairs. Can't you just leave this **one** area to me?"

While father and I faced each other, Sio Ying opened her door and peered out with a smirk on her lips. Then she turned her back on us, allowed the door to swing open wider and with deliberate slow motions swept up the broken pieces of porcelain. Father turned away, thinking the flare up was ended.

My shoulders slumped. When I turned to go, Sio Ying called out to me. "I walked into this house straight up and I'll leave flat."

I was defeated. I had thought I would win. Back in my room, I locked the door between father's room and mine. I closed my eyes and rested my forehead against the doorjamb. My heart thudded as I took deep breaths. Had it come to this? I turned around, leaned against the wall and stared at my image in the oval mirror across the room. I hissed my vow into the still room. "I will never to talk to Sio Ying or father again."

Chapter 18

After this tumultuous visit home, I returned to the university able to accept my estrangement from home. I planned to continue at the university after summer vacation, but it was not to be. In July 1937, the Japanese army that had been in northern China moved toward Shanghai, where they met weak resistance.

The largely ineffectual Chinese army consisted mainly of poor men, most of whom had joined up in order to get decent food and clothing. Other soldiers were strong young men who'd been forcibly torn from their poor families and made to serve. We had a saying, "Good men don't want to become soldiers, and good girls don't want to become prostitutes."

The Japanese moved into the eastern part of China, including Soochow and Shanghai. Well-to-do Chinese and others who refused to live under the Japanese packed up and fled to the interior of China. Soochow University closed and relocated to Chungking, southwest of Shanghai. Once the university buildings were vacated in Soochow, scavengers broke in and decimated the buildings and the dorms. I, like other students, lost everything, including my clothes, books, and even my good wool blanket. Later, the Japanese burned most of the university buildings.

During this period, my father's house, like others in the safe zones of the International Settlement and the French Concession, became overrun with relatives and friends. My friend Lucy, whose parents had moved to Hong Kong, stayed on at our home. One of father's wealthy friends, his three wives and three children, who had been living in a city outside of Shanghai, moved into the living quarters vacated by the Wongs. My mother's sister and her daughter fled from Wu Sih and took over what had formerly been the billiard room. Each of the families living in the house cooked and ate separately, but we occasionally got together for conversation or for games of mah-jongg.

People with no one to take them in were left to suffer under the Japanese. Buying or renting a place took a great deal of money. Some even talked about using gold bars to bribe homeowners to let them rent. Others who found housing, sub-rented part of the house at exorbitant fees. Food became harder to obtain; sugar, butter, eggs and refined rice were in short supply, but were available on the black market. Some people bought up scarce products like rice and candles and sold them for high prices. Food deliveries from father's land in Wu Sih, where the Japanese had firm control, stopped. If you had money, you could get what you needed, and for now, father's hotel supplied him with ready cash.

Although I lived at home again, I retained my vow of silence against Sio Ying and father. Auntie Yun and I were still on good terms. One morning I went to Auntie Yun's room while she was sewing and asked, "Auntie Yun, will you ask father for money for my next semester's books?"

She put down her sewing and looked at me with sad eyes. "You must talk to him. It is hurtful to him that you are silent."

Raising my chin and standing straighter, I announced, "Never as long as Sio Ying is in this house."

"You must try to get along with her," she pleaded.

"**You** have to get along, not I. Will you ask father for me?"

"You know he will give you anything."

"Will you be my intermediary?"

She nodded, just as I knew she would. Although the routine of requesting money from father was denigrating for Pun Yun, she would do almost anything for me.

With my schooling and my other financial needs taken care of, I went about my life as if nothing were amiss at home. Lucy and I took the bus to Kwong Wah, where Soochow University system had set up a "borrowed school." This move allowed students to transfer their credits from Soochow to the Kwong Wah campus, located in the Chinese section of Shanghai. Later, with the onset of the Japanese occupation of Shanghai, the school moved to the British International Settlement, where it rented buildings.

Summer in Shanghai could be stifling and with the anticipation of war the weather seemed more oppressive than ever. In 1937 Shanghai was caught between two armies, the Japanese and the Chinese Nationalist. During the first part of August, over ten thousand Chinese soldiers piled up sandbags around North Station. Japanese warships moved up the Whangpoo River. An evening of rain followed by clearing the next day left the air warm and sticky. We anticipated some shelling by the Japanese and were halfway prepared for it. However, it was the Chinese air force that first laid waste to the city. The air force had attempted to bomb the Japanese flagship, Idzumo, anchored in the river, but they inadvertently dropped bombs on the main streets of Shanghai. I was at home in the French Concession at the time, but heard the thunder, saw smoke, and cringed at the news that thousands of Chinese and foreigners had died. On Nanking Road, both the Palace and Cathay Hotels sustained heavy damage. I remained shielded from the conflict and caught only bits and pieces of the stories about the carnage.

We could see barbed wire from our area of the French Concession and hear the rat-a-tat of machine gun fire when thousands of Chinese troops resisted the oncoming Japanese forces. Still, most of us felt insulated from the conflict and believed we would be protected in our enclave. After all, it was only the inept Chinese air force that had caused the damage, not the Japanese.

On August 23rd the Nationalist troops fired at the Japanese on the river, but their shells fell on downtown Shanghai instead. Explosions tore into the Sincere Department store, and its walls caved in the side of the adjacent Wing On store. I heard about this from a bedraggled Lucy, who had been downtown during the attack. Soon afterward she rushed into my house. I took her up to my bedroom, got her a glass of water and tried to calm her down. At first she was incoherent, but gradually her sobs subsided enough for her to tell me what had happened.

"I was downtown when all of a sudden shells screamed over my head. I hid in a store. The noise was terrible." She held her hands to her ears as if the shelling were still going on. "Smoke and dust billowed up everywhere, but after a while I thought it was safe and went out onto Nanking Road. Bodies . . . they were all over. For a while I just stood there. I didn't know where to go. I walked over broken glass and crumbled masonry. A woman was sprawled across a man's body. Faces were unrecognizable, bodies torn, burned." Lucy buried her head in her hands as if trying to forget yet needing to talk. "A woman called out to me. A burning board lay on top of her chest. I looked away, but something made me turn back. It was Martha!"

"Martha? Yes. That's possible," I said. "She worked in the music department at Wing On."

"I tried to pick her burned clothing off her, but . . . ." Lucy gulped back tears. "She was badly burned. I stopped two workmen and begged them to help. They carried her to a nearby restaurant that had been set up as a Red Cross center. I left her in the care of a Chinese doctor. Oh, Tek, it was awful. I felt so helpless. I have no nursing skills, there was nothing else I could do. Can we get word to her family?"

Putting aside my resolve never to speak to my father again, I ran to father's study to tell him. He sent a servant to notify Martha's family. I went back to my room to try to comfort Lucy, but the trauma had left her trembling with fear. That night the distant bursts of fire seemed more real to me.

In October the Chinese soldiers retreated from Shanghai. Arbitrators from the Foreign Settlement made a pact with the Japanese, allowing the Japanese to march in and out of the area at will but without weapons. Outside the safe enclaves, the Japanese destroyed factories and workshops in Chapei and Hongkew and occupied those areas. They even tried to create a small Japan by keeping Hongkew on Japanese time—one hour ahead. Outside the foreign concession, the Japanese oversaw the destruction of Shanghai's international life by closing off trade, shutting down the dance halls, and outlawing "decadent" jazz.

With the Japanese occupation came curfews and barbed-wired barricades at the entrances to the International Settlement and the French Concession. At the barricades, we were ordered to bow, give a pleasant good morning then ask permission to continue. Most of the time, I, as well as the rest of the family, stayed inside our safe enclave and in particular stayed away from the infamous Garden Bridge that was the demarcation between the International Settlement and Hongkew. Because Father's third class hotel, the On Tong, in the International Settlement remained one of his sources of income, he traveled back and forth from Hongkew on business.

I heard the following story from Auntie Yun. One evening as father returned to the French Concession and began to cross the notorious Garden Bridge on the Hongkew side, the Japanese sentry stopped him.

"It's after ten," the sentry yelled.

Father looked at his watch and immediately realized his mistake. "I'm on China time," father said.

The guard marched toward him and slapped father's shoulder. "You're out after curfew. You're under arrest."

Before the guard could take father into custody, a car drove up, the window rolled down, and a familiar face leaned out into the night. A hand stretched out from the car to show the guard credentials. "Let him go," the voice said. "I know him. He's no trouble maker . . . only a small business man."

Father hustled away into the safe zone. Wong Yen Tai had returned to Shanghai, and for father it had been an opportune moment.

It was the beginning of a time when survival through whatever means was the rule of each day. The battle between the Chinese and Japanese secret services resulted in a number of street murders and assassinations in our area. If someone collaborated with the Japanese puppet government in Shanghai, he would soon be dead, cut down by "patriotic" gangs.

In this environment I continued my university studies.

In innocence and searching for elusive happiness, I was about to step out of my father's cage into a new cage I would design.

Chapter 19

Lucy's parents returned from Hong Kong in 1939. Housing was hard to find so they moved in with relatives, the Lambs. Lucy continued to live at our house.

"I always enjoy visiting with your father," I said to Lucy as we walked down the street to her parents' place after our classes at the Kwong Wah University.

"At least now that father's back in Shanghai, I don't spend my time writing letters to him in classical Chinese," she said.

"You loved writing them," I said.

"I didn't mind his red ink corrections, but sometimes he had re-written my entire letter." Lucy hugged her books to her chest.

"He adores you and has high hopes for you."

"So does your father," she said with a knowing look.

"It . . . it's not quite the same. You know how it is with my father and me." We continued walking side by side. "At least I have my boyfriend, Lee."

"He's charming, but a bit too self-confident for me," Lucy said.

I stopped in midstep and said, "He's quiet, not egotistical."

"I didn't say that." She thumped her books together. "You're taken with the way he dresses—
western suits and that elegant navy blue trench coat." She laughed, noticing my blushing cheeks.

"Better than the traditional blue Chinese gown most of the men students wear." I started to walk again and Lucy caught up to me. "His dress is very avant-garde."

Eventually we came to the house where Lucy's parents lived. Passing through a small garden, we entered the home. Lucy's father, Uncle To, came forward to greet us. He had a Japanese look about him, which enabled him to pass through the Japanese barricades without being asked any questions.

"We are rich with visitors today," Uncle To said. "You're just in time for tea. Lucy, your cousin Eddie is here."

Eddie Lamb's dark brown hair and a high, large nose gave him a foreign appearance, not unlike Europeans. He worked in the import department of a foreign-owned pharmacy. After a pleasant visit, I went on home and thought no more about Lucy's cousin. He was ten years older than I and appealed to me more as a brother than as a romantic possibility. Besides, no one could replace Lee in my eyes.

As time went on, whenever I visited the Tos, Eddie would be there. He would bring candy and take Lucy and me to the movies. Because Eddie was the sole support of his mother, his unmarried siblings, and an orphaned niece, he couldn't afford expensive dates. Most of the time he came over to my house, or we went to a chocolate shop where we would sit and talk.

Despite Eddie's attentions, I was enamored of Lee and thought he felt the same about me. One evening Lee and I sat in the parlor of my father's house, looking at western magazines. I was interested in the fashions, he in the cars.

"I saw one of those," he pointed to a La Salle, "in Hong Kong."

"It must be exciting to travel." I continued scanning the magazine for the latest fashions. "I'd like to do that someday."

"The export-import business isn't as good in Shanghai as I thought," Lee said. "I've got to go to Bangkok for at least a year."

I put down the magazine and stared at him. He was smiling as though he'd said nothing of importance. At first I thought he was joking, but that wasn't his style. "Business might be difficult in occupied China. But why Bangkok?" I asked, attempting to come to grips with this news.

"The rice business is thriving there. Here . . . " he shrugged. "Look, if I make money in a year, I'll come back. We can get together then."

"You're serious about this?" I edged away from him, feeling hot and miserable. My plans seemed to be unraveling. "Are you sure you'll do well in Bangkok?"

"You know what they say. It might be like trying to find a pin in the ocean, but I want to give it a try. If I don't return, forget about me."

I was stunned, both by his nonchalant attitude and his belief that our interest in each other could so easily be put off. But I convinced myself that he'd return to me and Shanghai in a year's time. My focus on Lee wouldn't allow me to think otherwise; after all I'd always gotten what I wanted and I wanted Lee.

* * *

After Lee left town, I continued my studies, dated other fellows and enjoyed the company of Eddie Lamb. Finally in 1940 I accomplished my father's and my goal by finishing my studies at the University. Through my college years, for the most part, I'd retained my vow of silence against father. Yet I wanted him to show his approval of my success by coming to my graduation ceremony. How could I weaken and ask him? Only my dear friend, Lucy, would watch me receive my degree.

When I walked down the aisle of the Grand Theater to receive my diploma, along with the graduates from five missionary schools—St. John's, Shanghai, Soochow, Hangchow, and Nanking, I spotted father sitting next to Lucy. I smiled, thankful that she had taken it upon herself to invite him. After the ceremony as I walked toward them in the crowded lobby, I thought of the years of silence between us. At home I'd been aware of him only by his footsteps on the stairs, the sound of his voice, the wafting of his cigar smoke as he passed my room, or the rumbling of his car engine as he left or returned home. Now we were face to face and he looked stern. I stood before him with a blank expression, unable to utter a word.

"Let's go to the Ching Kung restaurant," Lucy said, breaking the tense silence.

On the short drive to the restaurant no one spoke. All through the dinner while we ate a special duck dish, the conversation was mundane, halting. Even on the drive home our conversation remained stilted. Neither father nor I knew how to broach the years of silence, yet my self-inflicted exile from my father had cracked, allowing a healing process to begin.

Upon our return home, father gathered his immediate family in the western-style living room. Our other cousins, aunties, and uncles milled around in the hall outside the great room, knowing something important was to be announced. Sio Ying's smile should have warned me. Although I'd made peace with father, my vow of silence with Sio Ying remained.

Father sat in his favorite chair, looked out upon his audience and announced, "I'm selling the house."

There was a hissing intake of breath from the relatives and a murmuring in the hall. I looked at

Auntie Yun, who was so startled by the news that she clasped her hands together over her heart. I nodded knowingly to myself. Sio Ying knew of the coming sale, but not Auntie Yun.

"With these difficult times, it was an offer I couldn't refuse," father continued.

Inside my head, I heard my voice cry out, no, no, you can't do this, but I only asked, "Who's buying it?"

"An American Jew. A real estate broker," father said. "I've found a smaller place in Eden Village."

Our relatives' faces grew long and troubled; our house had been their shelter. "What of us?" one of my uncles asked, gesturing to those who listened with anxious faces.

"All has been arranged." Father ignored the scowls from the group in the hall. He had been their benefactor for so long that they assumed he would take care of them forever. "Don't worry. I'll see that each family is settled. No one will be homeless." He motioned for them to disband.

After the group in the hall began to disperse, father continued. "Some of this furniture will go to them," he nodded toward his retreating relatives; "the new place can't hold all this." He rose from his chair. "The new owner admired the polished rosewood and inlaid marble tables and chairs," he said, running his fingers along the edge of one of the tables. "I included them in the price of the house." He smiled at Sio Ying, then turned to Auntie Yun. "Don't be downcast. Tomorrow we will visit our new home and you may chose your room."

I looked at Sio Ying's rapturous face. It was obvious to me that this move would allow her to get out from under the rest of the relatives, who had never respected nor befriended her. She was only Lau Ya's mistress, a fact no one ever let her forget. Even her son tormented her with this fact whenever he made his infrequent visits to our home.

The following day we drove to our new three-storied

home. It faced Eden Road and abutted the big, iron gate which opened into the village of twenty homes. Our private gate led off the street into the front garden of our house. Inside, father showed us the room he had chosen for himself, the smallest bedroom on the second floor.

"Now, Pun Yun, you must chose the bedroom you would like," father said.

I smiled fondly at father, knowing he was trying to make up to Auntie Yun for taking her away from the grand house. Choosing her bedroom was not a minor decision, for the competition with Sio Ying was a factor, and each one's prestige was at stake. The direction the room faced was important. The fronts of Chinese houses were always built facing south. If the house faced north, bad luck was in the offing. This belief had much to do with the weather and the rising and setting of the sun, and choosing the right exposure assured its occupant good fortune. Auntie Yun inspected first the large west-facing room, then the smaller east-facing one, which over-looked the garden and the street. Traditionally the east-facing room was the first wife's.

She hesitated briefly, then said, "I'll take the east-facing room."

Sio Ying was delighted to have the large west-facing room, a much grander one than the small guestroom she'd occupied in the old house. My room was the largest east-facing room on the third floor. I easily accepted the distribution, but the location of the staircase bothered me. I would now have to pass by Sio Ying's door every time I went to my room. But I could say nothing, Sio Ying had won before and she would win again if I asked father to keep the old house.

Despite the occupation and the war, I was in the flower of my youth, enjoying a social life with several men. My family's struggles seemed less important than my self-absorbed life of men, parties, and friends. Little did I know that one day I, too, would pay the price that history extracts from each of us.

While waiting for Lee's return from Bangkok, I dated both Eddie and a boy named Pond, who wore fancy white sharkskin suits and black and white spectator shoes. Lucy, I, Eddie and Jack Chen, a long time friend of Eddie's, went dancing together, held gatherings at our house, and drove to the Aristocrat Chocolate Shop, a nearby westernized coffee house for coffee, sodas or ice cream. In those days, we regarded anything American as wonderful.

For the first few years of the Japanese occupation, we had no idea what was happening to father's land around Wu Sih. Then one day the land manager, Lok Hsiao-ming arrived at our new home. Lok's gray quilted gown drooped from his slim frame, his homemade black cotton shoes were tattered and his black skullcap sat askew on his head. Yet he had remained the same sensible man father had hired so many years before. We were delighted and surprised that he'd made it not only to Shanghai but into the French Concession. He had brought us a few pounds of fresh vegetables on a cart. The Japanese had confiscated some of the food he'd planned to bring, but they'd left enough to make the trip worthwhile.

"How's my land?" father asked, sitting down in his favorite chair in the living room, while Hsiao-ming stood inside the archway leading from the hall.

"The dirt's still there; the vegetables grow; the houses are standing, but they've sustained a lot of damage. At first the Japanese ransacked everything; then some order was restored. Now they take only a percentage of what we grow. This is the first time I've been able to travel outside of Wu Sih."

"What of your family?" I asked, thinking of his daughter whom I had played with as a youngster.

"I sent my wife and daughter to Chongqing before the Japanese came in '37'."

"Have you heard from them since?" Auntie Yun asked from across the room, where she sat in a small straight-backed chair.

"Once a year a message gets through. They are well, but Chongqing is crowded with refugees, and the Japanese continue their bombing raids."

"I'm delighted you were able to make it into Shanghai," father said. "I have had some problems with the Japanese at the bridge." Father stared into the distant corner of the room, and I wondered if he were thinking about his old "friend" Yen Tai. Could father forgive him for working for the Japanese?

Apparently Auntie Yun also remembered the Yen Tai bridge incident and asked, "What about Hai Li?"

Lok shrugged. "I don't know. I've heard nothing of her, but if Wong Yen Tai has a position with the Japanese, she's well off."

Although we had learned little about Hai Li, we did have the good news that Lok Hsiao-ming's family was safe. We knew we probably wouldn't see him for some time. We wished him well and watched him trudge down the street with his now empty cart.

We had to accept that father's land had been lost with the occupation.

No one's business or farm was assured of surviving. There was nothing father could do but operate his hotel and secure as many business deals and property management arrangements as he could. Even in wartime, business must continue if people are to survive.

Chapter 20

1942–1944

A year had passed since Lee Chou had left for Bangkok. Maria, my old friend from college and I sat gossiping in my room on her Sunday off from her job. Suddenly, she dropped the bombshell. "I saw your old friend Chou at the Park Hotel's dining room last night."

"Back in town!" I said and jumped up from my rosewood desk where I'd been doodling as the two of us talked. I tried to cover up my surprise. I couldn't let her know how I really felt about him. "Oh. Well, that's nice. How's he doing?"

"He's no good for you," Maria said.

"Did he just get into town?" I didn't know what else to say.

"I . . . I don't think so. Forget him, Tek."

Forget him? Impossible. Why hadn't he rung me up or come over to the house? Why? "Maybe his job didn't work out in Bangkok and he's ashamed."

"I was told he'd made a good deal of money," Maria said reluctantly.

I was tongue-tied. What was keeping him from calling?

The rest of Maria's visit was a blur. All I could think about was Lee. She left early, perhaps realizing I wasn't fit company while I stewed about Lee. Two weeks later when Auntie Yun answered the phone and told me Lee Chou was on the line, I rushed into the study and grabbed the phone from her.

"I heard you were in town," I said, trying to keep my voice under control.

"I didn't want to bother you...."

"What?" I gripped the phone tighter.

"I'm going to Canada to further my education."

"I heard you did well in Thailand." Could I keep the hurt out of my voice?

"That's why I'm off to Canada. It's a great opportunity."

"What am I to think?" I twisted the phone cord around my fingers.

"Tek, I'm really looking forward to seeing Canada."

"I'm sure you are."

"I'll write from Canada. Take care."

The phone went dead before I had a chance to respond. I put the phone on the cradle, closed my eyes, and cried. For weeks afterwards, I went over and over our conversation in my mind. My friends tried to console me, but nothing helped. One day Lucy came to my house, took my hand and had me sit down on my bed. Standing over me, she said, "You might as well hear the truth. Lee didn't go to Canada after all. He's rented a room at a boarding house."

"Why hasn't he called then?"

"Tek. Are you blind? He would have called if he were interested in you. Forget him. Eddie likes you. Why don't you pay more attention to him?"

"I don't love Eddie." She couldn't understand how much I wanted Lee!

"Lee doesn't want you."

"He does. He's just... just... I know what I'll do. It's his thirtieth birthday soon. I'll buy him a tie and a card and take it to him."

"You're crazy!" Lucy said. "It's not proper for you to go alone."

"You'll come with me won't you?"

"Never. You'll just make a fool of yourself."

"Fine friend you are. I'll ask Martha." Ever since Martha had recovered from her burns, she and I had done more things together.

On the appointed day I almost ran to Chou's boarding house, Martha following at my heels. At the front of the building, I stopped abruptly, causing Martha to bump into me. "What's the matter?" she asked.

"Nothing," I lied. I didn't want her to know I had doubts about what I was doing. "I just want to be sure this is the right place." Hesitantly, we climbed the steps to the building. Just inside the front hall, I spotted a friend of Lee's coming down the staircase. "It's all right," I whispered to Martha. "I know him."

"I've come to deliver a package to Lee," I told him.

"It's not a good idea for you to be here. Anyway, Lee's not here now," he said.

"I just want to leave this present for him in his room."

He looked at Martha and me and shrugged. After getting the key from the office, he showed us the way to Lee's room and unlocked the door. "Look, I've got to run. Just leave the gift and go. I don't think he'll be back for a while. You do know all about Lee don't you? I mean, I'd hate to see someone like you get mixed up with the guy."

His warning made me think of how Lee had lied to me about going to Canada, but I pushed those thoughts from my mind. After Lee's friend left, I stepped into the room alone and walked over to the desk to leave my gift and card. Upon seeing the pictures on his desk, I knew I'd made a mistake. Although my picture was there, it stood next to several other pictures of him drinking and partying with other women. One in particular caught my eye—a picture of a cheap-looking Portuguese dance hall girl from the Paramount Dance Hall. The signs were everywhere in the room. A lace beige slip hung over the side of the bed, and perfume bottles stood on a side table. She was obviously living with him. I snatched up my gift and card and stormed out of the room, marching right by a surprised Martha, who was waiting outside the door.

Of course, Lee's friend told him I'd been there, and Lee called me with his pitiful excuse; he was only helping the girl out because she had no where else to stay.

"You don't need to explain to me," My voice was flat as I fiddled with my necklace. "I have nothing to say to you." I banged the phone down. "Rake!" I shouted to no one and began to cry.

Finding out about Lee's affair intensified my reckless dating—Pond, Eddie and almost anyone who asked me out. When Pond and Eddie became serious about me, I was thrilled. Chou had been a fool to treat me as he had. Pond, knowing that I didn't approve of his wavy pompadour, cut his hair just to please me. Eddie, too, went out of his way to please me—to the point that he annoyed me; he was too nice and too agreeable. Every time he came to see me he brought chocolates and fruit.

One day he came to the house and presented me with a beautiful leather handbag. I blurted out, "You have no right to think I'd accept an expensive gift from you." I threw the purse at him and strode out of the room.

While I was acting like a spoiled child toward Eddie, Lee continued to call, but never sent me gifts or flowers, nor asked me out. Instead he pursued me by phone. "I know Pond's cut his hair just for you," he said. "He's not for you. I'll break his puny neck. I saw you first. I'll lose face if you keep seeing him."

"That's absurd," I said. "You wronged me, not the other way around." I waited for him to argue with me. But silence greeted my accusation, and I slammed the phone down. I collapsed in a nearby chair and sat moping for a long time.

Soon after this impossible conversation, I received a letter from Eddie. "Dear Tek," he wrote. "I'm asking you to marry me. Please do me the honor of answering with a simple yes or no."

What was Eddie thinking? I wasn't interested in him. I tore off the lower half of the letter and wrote, "NO!" and sent the answer back to him. I thought that would end it, but Eddie proposed to me a second time. When I again said, "no," my friends shook their heads.

"Why are you so nasty to Eddie?" Maria asked. "He's independent now so you won't have to worry about living with his family after you marry. He's got an excellent job and makes good money."

"And he loves you so much you could do whatever you wanted to do," Lucy said.

"All right! All right!" I said, throwing up my hands. "I might marry him, but only because I could wear a beautiful wedding gown." I immediately thought of what the gown would look like, lace and fine silk. I saw myself twirling under lights with admiring glances following my every move.

When Eddie proposed a third time, I said, "yes."

He was so happy he bought me not one, but several records of the Andrew Sisters' singing "I'll Be With You In Apple Blossom Time," and played them over and over again. After a time, I would rush out of the room covering my ears with my hands when he played that record. He lavished me with jewelry, bringing me diamonds from a diamond dealer and letting me choose the ones I wanted.

"I'll have a brooch made with seven of the diamonds," Eddie said.

"I'll design the earrings to match the brooch," I said, thinking that since I was giving up my single life to marry Eddie, I deserved such gifts. Eddie would seal our engagement with a four-carat diamond ring and enough mink skins to make into a coat. Another girl would have been excited anticipating the gifts, but since I didn't love Eddie, I found the entire matter boring, although I was glad to have the gifts.

As soon as the jewelry was ready, Eddie and his friend, Jack Chen, would come over to present the engagement ring and gifts. When I told father Eddie would be announcing our engagement, father seemed pleased, but in a rather reserved manner. Had he thought I would never marry? Then without confiding in me, father planned a dinner party.

I hadn't thought to get a proper engagement dress, which was the traditional thing to do. When I found out about father's engagement party plans, I called up Lucy and the two of us raced out to shop for a dress for the evening.

"I don't understand you," Lucy said, watching me try on one dress after another. "You're reactions to Eddie's gifts are so strange. You haven't planned anything. You asked your friends to the party at the last minute."

"I didn't know father was going to give a party."

"You knew he would. Most girls would have planned ahead to buy a special dress for their engagement. They would have discussed the party with their father and mother."

I ignored her. Of course she was right, but I wasn't thrilled about what I had gotten myself into. I picked out a ready-made black velvet dress trimmed with gold sequins and beads, and had it wrapped; then Lucy and I dashed home in time for the party.

Normally, the main gate remained closed and family members entered our home through the back door. But because our engagement was a special occasion, the servant opened the main gate. Eddie and Jack came in through the garden and front door, carrying the jewel box containing the diamonds and the box holding the mink skins. Father welcomed them in the Chinese style living room with its straight-backed chairs, large carved table and Chinese wall hangings. Jack and Eddie placed the gifts on the small wooden table next to where father stood. By presenting the gifts in this manner, they were respectfully telling my father that Eddie wanted to marry me. I flinched when Eddie moved closer so he could slip the large glittering four-carat ring on my finger. I felt like a queen receiving booty. The ring did look stunning on my hand. With a serious expression, father bowed his head, acknowledging his agreement to the coming marriage. Together Eddie and I bowed to my father. Father and Eddie exchanged a few cordial words, saying they were pleased about the coming union. Then Eddie and Jack left.

Friends and relatives invited to the dinner party came in the early evening to view the engagement gifts before dinner. The diamond jewelry was laid out in a green velvet box, and the mink skins were draped across the back of the dark mahogany table. Mah-jongg and poker games went on before and after dinner. The party lasted until midnight with laughter and merriment. Music played, and I felt gay and lighthearted. Eddie, as was the custom, was not at the party. This bothered me very little.

In early March 1943, our engagement became official and now we had to find a place to live. Eddie and I went to look for an apartment, and I always asked one of my girl friends to come with us. It was as if I shunned any kind of intimacy with him. I'd never lived in an apartment and when I saw how small they were, I was stunned. How could I live in such close quarters with a man I didn't love?

"Eddie," I complained, after we walked out of the sixth apartment we'd looked at, "I hate it. It's so small. Do you want to smother me?"

Maria, who stood next to me whispered, "I like it. It's nice."

"Then you live in it with Eddie," I hissed back at her.

"It's not easy with the housing shortage." Eddie looked back at the apartment house.

"I said I'd marry you, but I didn't say I'd live in a box. I'm not going to settle for just any place."

We stood in the street arguing until Maria intervened. "Maybe there's a solution. I heard the Japanese have ordered the foreign community out of Shanghai. They'll be forced to sell at low prices."

Eddie nodded. "I heard the same thing. Most of them, excluding Germans and the other wartime allies of the Japanese, are to be sent to concentration camps in central China. It's awful. But since it's happened, it might help us. I'll check it out." With that we stopped looking at rental apartments.

What Eddie and Maria had heard occurred in late March 1943. In mid-May the Jews were evacuated, not to concentration camps, but to a ghetto in Hongkew. Over 16,000 Jews organized themselves into what we Chinese called a *baojia*, a secure zone for whites from overseas that they self-governed. However, the Jews were at the mercy of the Japanese guards. In an ironic twist, the head Japanese officer gave himself the title: "King of the Jews."

Since foreigners had been banished from the French Concession, Eddie was able to find and purchase a small house near my father's house. This house had been designed by a French architect, and no space had been wasted. We had no front or back yard, since the house filled a tiny triangular piece of land. The house contained a living room, dining area, a bedroom with a sun porch, a study, a garage and servants' quarters with a storage area. I called it the tiniest house in Shanghai, but I was willing to live there with Eddie.

My ancestors, accustomed to arranged marriages, would

think nothing of this loveless marriage, but the emptiness was not what I had expected. I was making my own cage in a hapless manner. Would I be sorry later?

Chapter 21

1944

Now that Eddie and I had a place to live, I brightened up at the thought of shopping for my dowry. Since father had bought diamonds and jewelry for Gun Yuen's bride when they married, I felt there should be no limits set on what I could spend; father would pay for whatever I wanted.

According to the old custom, a prospective bride showed that she was bringing a rich dowry to the marriage by the number of comforters–*be duhs*–she purchased. Friends would ask, "How many *be duhs* does she have?" and relatives, especially mothers-in-law and sisters-in-laws, would be pleased in proportion to the number of *be duhs* the bride exhibited after the marriage. To be rich enough to have 48 *be duhs* piled on the bed up to the ceiling was the ideal. While observing the custom, I had a more realistic and modern view; I reduced the number of *be duhs* I bought to sixteen.

Shopping for the embroidered silk covers–*be mes*–took

Lucy and me to a street where each shop sold nothing but embroidered silk comforter covers and embroidered clothing. We went to one store after another examining the piles of colorful *be mes*.

"Look at this one," Lucy said, holding up a Chinese red *be me*.

"I hate that color," I replied.

"But you have to have one in this color to symbolize your wedding."

I didn't want to hear her protest. "At least I found eight in multi-colored pastels that I like. Now I need only eight more."

"Tek, we've already been to five stores and you haven't found what you want."

"Let's go back to the first shop. I think they had the best I've seen so far."

Eventually I found eight more *be mes* in shades of light pink, blue, beige, apple green, and turquoise and had the sales people wrap them up. Later I sent Ah Gan to pick them up.

Auntie Yun had the job of sewing the comforters into the *be mes*. She searched for a lady (a *Fok Chee Tai Tai*, meaning, "All perfect lucky Mrs." . . .) who would help her sew them. No widow or single woman would do; the lady had to be married, with a good husband, good sons, and good grandchildren to have *fok chee*. If both her parents or in-laws were still alive, the woman had even more *fok chee*.

The *Fok Chee Tai Tai* Auntie Yun found turned out to be a relative. After Auntie Yun had picked a lucky day from a Chinese fortune book, she asked the *Fok Chee Tai Tai* to come to our house on that day for a little party and a day of sewing. The *Fok Chee Tai Tai* and Auntie Yun sat on chairs surrounded by piles of material. They sipped tea and busily sewed the whole day. I stopped in to watch them and was fascinated by the scene. With each stitch, their hands and arms created a rhythm. Like synchronized clocks they swayed back and forth chatting and chanting over and over and over, "*Tuo Tzi Two Sun*—Have lots of sons, lots of grandchildren."

I ran out of the house that day.

My next shopping spree brought me to the Silver Chamber Shop, located between two silk shops on Nanking Road. I had often admired the elaborate Chinese filigree decorating the outside of its top floor. The displays inside were a treasure trove. I browsed through the store and eventually bought silverware with silver bowls and pairs of silver chopsticks. For special occasions I picked out a large nine-sectioned pumpkin-shaped silver bowl decorated with leaves and tendrils. This would be used at my tea table, surrounded by footed dishes for fruit or candies.

I was too proud to ask father for money, so I just sent what I had bought to his hotel in his name. Father's accountant would pay for all my purchases. Besides the items I purchased, father completed my dowry with a set of porcelain Chinese dishes, as well as a set of everyday dishes, a set of knives, forks, spoons, two camphor chests for woolens, and silver cups used for tooth brushing.

This whirlwind of shopping made me dismiss any reservations I had about marrying Eddie. I was enjoying this part of getting married and wanted to share it. On the way to shop for my wedding dress I stopped by Maria's. As we chatted outside her house, I gloried in the beautiful day and what lay ahead of me. "Do you want to come with me?" I asked.

"Who are you going to have make your dress?"

"Madame Garnet, of course."

"Haughty Madame Garnet! I thought the Japanese had ordered her to leave along with all the other foreigners."

"She's a French Russian. Maybe that's why they let her stay on. She's still located in that expensive shop of hers. I wonder if she'll be as snobbish as before?"

Maria shrugged. "I'll go with you just to see what she's like now."

The two of us hurried off down the street, I with excitement, Maria with curiosity. Inside Madame Garnet's fancy shop, one of her helpers greeted us. "I've come to order my wedding dress," I said with pride. "May I look at one of your magazines to see what style I'd like?"

Madame Garnet had been sitting in a corner ignoring Maria and me, but when she heard my request, she rose and approached us. She looked me up and down, drew herself up on her sandled feet with her little red manicured toes sticking out and said, "You come to me for a wedding dress. I will select the design that best suits you. You don't know what would look best on you."

This insult drained away my enthusiasm as though I'd been turned inside out. Cowed, I stood there not knowing what to say. But if I wanted Madame Garnet to make my dress, I'd have to accept whatever she decreed. She had the best reputation and I wanted the best. I bought the fourteen yards of white brocaded satin she said she would need to make the gown. She provided the waist length veil. On her advice and despite my aversion to red, I ordered red roses for my bridal bouquet. I'd also wear a few of them at my waist during the dancing after the wedding ceremony. I thought red roses an odd choice, but didn't dare question Madame.

My finished wedding gown was very simple; it had a small removable cape and a wide sash. I wondered about Madame Garnet. Had I really needed fourteen yards of material for this? The veil was similar to a nun's veil, but with ruffled edges. Next came fittings for my trousseau. For this part of my trousseau, a tailor came to our house, measured me and made several cheongsams, both short and long. These were the traditional one-piece dresses with Chinese collars and side-slit skirts. For my going away dress, the tailor made a turquoise velvet cheongsam that I would wear with a diamond broach Eddie had given me. My outfit would be enhanced with white camellias in my hair.

During the time I was wrapped up in the excitement of my trousseau, dowry and wedding dress, I never thought of Eddie. A few weeks before the wedding while I was taking inventory of my wardrobe, Maria burst into my bedroom. "Have you heard about Eddie? He's got an ulcer. They might have to operate!" She sat on a chair next to my bed. "Didn't you hear me? He's in the hospital. When will you visit him?"

"I'm too busy." I continued examining the dresses in my wardrobe. "He can't be that sick." I pulled out an old dress and threw it on the bed. "Too old-fashioned. I'll let Sun Mei have it."

"He's going to be your husband." Maria's voice sounded louder than usual. "Don't you care?"

"No!" How inconvenient that he's ill, I thought. "I'll send him flowers."

With Maria's urging, I accompanied her to the florist shop. "Pick out violets," she said. Violets in a basket signified a swift recovery, so I agreed with her choice, paid the shopkeeper and turned to leave.

"What about a card?" the shopkeeper asked with a questioning smile on her round face.

I shrugged. Maria picked out a card and handed it to me. "You sign it for me, will you please?" I said and flounced out of the shop.

Maria's eyes had narrowed into slits when she joined me outside on the street. "I know I was among those who talked you into marrying Eddie, but maybe it wasn't such a good idea. You mustn't treat him this way."

"What way? I'm doing everything I'm supposed to do before a wedding."

"Everything but care for Eddie." Her usual sweet mouth pursed into a thin line.

"It's not my fault he's sick. You go visit him if you care so much. Just don't catch what he's got or you won't be in the wedding party."

She pulled back and glared at me. "Ulcers aren't catching, but they can be dangerous."

"He'll be fine. He wouldn't want me to see him looking peaked anyway. The wedding will go on as planned. That's what he and everyone wants isn't it?"

Maria turned and walked away, leaving me alone on the street. "He'll be fine," I called after her.

That same afternoon Lee called and finally urged me to go out with him. I didn't see any reason why I shouldn't. We went to a local dance hall, but even before we had our first dance, Lee asked, "Why do you want to marry Eddie?"

"What a question. I'm getting married in a week."

"That doesn't mean anything." He leaned close to me inspecting my face. "Why are you doing it?"

I turned away. "It's too late to change my plans. Aren't we going to dance?"

"You aren't making any sense." He put his hand on my arm. "What do you see in him?"

I stared at his hand. "He asked me to marry him. Listen, the music is excellent; we shouldn't miss a beat."

We moved onto the dance floor. And as we twirled around, he kept questioning me. "Why did you accept?"

I pulled back and asked, "Where were you when I accepted Eddie's proposal?"

He didn't answer, but the picture of his dance hall hussy came into my mind. It was his fault I was getting married to someone else, not mine. The rhythm of the music died in my heart. Each dance became more and more of an effort. My feet moved to the music while I parried each of his probing questions. After Lee dropped me off at home, I climbed the stairs to my room and flung myself on my bed and wept.

On the day of my wedding, Maria and my friend, Vera, came to help me dress for the ceremony and the bridal picture-taking. After I donned my exquisite gown and veil, I looked at myself in the mirror. I had never looked lovelier. So why wasn't I happy? I tried to smile at my friends, but my lips trembled and my smile turned into a grimace. Maria and Vera looked at each other and back at me and shook their heads.

"You should be very happy today." Maria said.

"I am. It's going to be a beautiful wedding with all my friends around me."

"We'll always be friends, Tek. Marriage won't change that," Vera said.

"You're right. Everything will be the same. After all I'm only getting married." My words still didn't make my marriage seem real. I headed out the door with my friends trailing behind and hurried down to the second floor, then halted. Below at the bottom of the stairs at the door to our living room, father and Auntie Yun stood waiting. Father was dressed in his Chinese "Tux," a long navy blue silk brocade gown topped by a black brocade *ma qua*. Auntie Yun wore a wine-colored brocade cheongsam. Father glanced up with shining admiration. How could I not go through with the wedding? My role-playing had gone too far. There was no turning back.

I stepped down the stairs until I faced them. I kowtowed to them as a way of saying "thanks for my life and now I bid you good-bye." Then I rose and moved into the living room and over to the corner where my mother's spirit seat was located. Thick stubby lighted candles nestled in front of it, flickering shadows onto the wall. For a fraction of a second I imagined the dancing shadows to be my mother's ghost. The sweet scent of burning incense curled into the air. Here before mother's spirit seat, I again kowtowed in respect to my mother and my ancestors. Tears misted my eyes, but I blinked them back, rose from my kneeling position and left the house for the photo appointment scheduled to take place before the wedding service.

At the Skversky photo studio while Russian Mr. Skversky fussed over me and moved me into one pose after another, I smiled, enjoying my role as a bride.

Mr. Skversky fumed. "You smile with your face, not with your eyes. A smile should come from deep inside on a day like today."

I smiled wider, but he frowned and muttered. "You're a bride. Happy! I need a happy photo. I can't make a picture come to life if the model is so, so . . . ." He slapped his hands to his side in frustration.

I shrugged and looked over at Vera and Maria who were waiting patiently after we'd had our pictures taken together. Eventually, Mr. Skversky finished taking pictures, but he kept muttering to himself. "Not a happy picture. Why does a bride make it so difficult for me? They won't like the pictures. Such a stilted smile."

The moment Eddie walked into the studio for the bride and groom picture, even my "stilted" smile faded. Still recuperating from his illness, he looked thin, his skin waxen. How dare he look so sickly on this day. While Eddie and I posed together, perspiration beaded Mr. Skversky's brow and his jowls flapped. "A nice smile, please. Please! One smile. This is a happy occasion. Please smile!" I stood like a tree, but refused to smile.

He took the picture, shaking his massive head. Maria and Vera looked at each other and they, too, shook their heads. Eddie gave a wan smile, but I could not and would not oblige with even a hint of pleasure in my upcoming marriage.

Later that day over 500 people attended our wedding and the reception, both of which were held at the Park Hotel across from the Shanghai racetrack in the International Settlement. To the strains of Lohengrin's wedding march, I walked down the aisle on my father's arm. Eddie's favorite niece, my flower girl, spread flowers in our path. At the table located at the end of the room, Eddie, dressed in a western tuxedo, waited for me. We signed the wedding certificate, and a Bank Director father knew said a few words. How far I had come from the traditional Chinese wedding.

Because our wedding took place during the Japanese occupation, we served only an afternoon tea after the ceremony. An orchestra played dance music, and Eddie and I moved onto the dance floor. I could feel his thin shoulders as we came together to dance the first dance. He was too weak to do more than a slow fox trot; he couldn't manage the waltz I longed to dance. After that first dance, he sat down. For the rest of the afternoon, I danced waltzes and tangos with other men, swirling about and enjoying every moment of being admired by others. But the joyful afternoon vanished as if it were a dream. All too soon it was time for me to change into my going-away outfit.

That evening Eddie's close friends and relatives came to our new tiny house for dinner. According to tradition, this dinner never included the bride's family. But it wasn't proper for the bride to be at the dinner by herself, so Vera and Marie, who were my bridal attendants, joined me. Later that night after everyone had left, I felt uncomfortable with Eddie in the bedroom, for I was a virgin and had never even kissed him. We kissed and Eddie made affectionate overtures, but I remained a virgin that night. He was still too ill and too weak. I was elated that my wedding night was a celibate night. How odd that my parents' history should repeat itself, albeit for different reasons.

The following morning we paid Eddie's mother the customary visit to show our respect to her and Eddie's ancestors. Upon entering her house, we were shown into a western style living room where Eddie's mother awaited us. Her imposing tall build dictated by her mixed Scottish and Chinese heritage somewhat intimidated me. First, Eddie and I bowed to the spirit seat of his ancestors, indicating that I had joined his family as a dutiful wife. As I bowed, Eddie's mother pushed my head sharply lower. Apparently, I hadn't bowed low enough to suit her. Was this her way of asserting her dominance over me? After I bowed lower, she smiled. Perhaps I was suitable after all. Eddie and I then turned and bowed to her.

This ritual completed, she led us to another corner of the room and showed her acceptance of me as her son's wife by giving me a jade and diamond bracelet. I thanked her and in turn gave her a pair of embroidered pillowcases and a *be me* to show my respect for her. It was a stiff and formal meeting with little warmth or conversation, but we were expected to follow tradition.

As custom decreed, Eddie and I visited my father at my former family home on the third day after our wedding. Father threw a party, with all our relatives there to honor us. Eddie's mother brought a whole roasted baby pig. This signified that the bride had been a virgin, thus bringing honor to the bride's family. What would Eddie's mother have thought if she'd known the truth of our first few married nights?

My Cantonese maid, Ah Yuh, whom Lucy had found for me, accompanied us. I was pleased with the way Ah Yuh looked, her black hair pulled back and plaited into a long braid and her uniform of wide black trousers, black shoes, and white jacket. After Eddie and I settled into the living room, Ah Yuh carried in stacks of containers holding the special bland food for Eddie prepared by a cook Eddie's mother had sent to live with us. It hadn't occurred to me that he needed a special diet, but then I'd pretended his illness was irrelevant to my life.

During the evening, father took Eddie aside and I knew his questioning would show his concern for me and my welfare. "Why do you work for someone else?" he asked Eddie. "Working for yourself is better."

Eddie agreed, but noted that he didn't have enough money to buy a pharmacy of his own at this time.

"I'll find one for you. You operate it and I'll be the silent partner."

True to his word, father found a pharmacy in the French Concession, bought it, and renamed it the South Sea Pharmacy, installing Eddie as manager and pharmacist.

I'd had the excitement of planning for our marriage, the ceremony was over, we had a house and Eddie had a new position. Would this self-made cage bring me happiness?

Chapter 22

At first our married life was comfortable; Eddie and I were friends. We didn't make love, for he remained impotent from his ulcer medication. Eddie worked at the pharmacy, and we invited friends over on weekends. I visited teahouses with friends and had an easy time at home with a maid and a cook.

During one of my outings to a teahouse with Maria and Lucy, Maria asked, "When are you and Eddie going to have children?"

"We just got married. Give us time."

"Eddie will be a wonderful father," Lucy said. "And you will be a good mother," she added almost as an after thought.

"Eddie's very busy at work," I said.

"You do want children don't you?" Maria asked.

"Sure." I looked out over the crowd, avoiding her eyes and changing the subject. "Remember all the wonderful shopping we did. It seems years ago." I sighed. We left the teahouse and went our separate ways. Maria's questioning started me thinking. It had been almost six months since

Eddie and I married, and I was still a virgin. Was he worthless as a man?

One day Eddie invited a friend, Mrs. Yong, her sister, and Mrs. Yong's daughter, Mildred, to dinner. But instead of Mildred's arriving with her mother, Mildred's boyfriend, Willie, showed up in her place.

"You are kind to include me," the tall, dark, handsome Willie said. "It's a pleasure to visit your home. I don't get out much because of my studies. I'm an engineering student at St. John's."

"It's nice you came. Eddie would have been outnumbered otherwise." I said. During dinner the women chatted easily with Eddie, while Willie, who sat next to me, and I enjoyed a discussion about university life. My heart beat faster and I could feel my cheeks glowing.

"You and Eddie have a lovely home," Mrs. Yong said, interrupting Willie's discourse about one of his classes.

"I'm certain it's smaller than you're used to," I said.

"It's dimensions are perfect," Eddie said. "The architect was a Frenchman. Very well known."

"He used up every inch of the ground for the house so there's no garden," I countered. Willie watched me from under his dark lashes. How perceptive was he about Eddie's and my relationship?

After everyone had left, Eddie approached me. "When we have guests, we shouldn't disagree. We should show a common front."

"I only said the house was smaller than most."

"I didn't mean that. I meant that you spent all your time talking to Willie."

"But you spent all your time talking to the women. What else could I do? It would have been impolite not to have conversed about things of interest to him."

The very next day Willie phoned me and asked if he could visit me. Without hesitating, I said yes. His visit was to be the first of many. I was drawn to Willie like a fish swimming upstream to find home. When I was with him, I felt free, happy. I realized I was at last in love with someone. He moved out of Mrs. Yong's home and rented a room near my house. Almost every day we were together, going to the movies or a teahouse to dance or just walking and window-shopping.

One mild sunny day we rode our bicycles over to my father's house. I had told Willie that my father had once been chief of an arsenal, and Willie, too, had an interest in weapon engineering. Once father and Willie had talked about weapons, father left the room and returned with a role of paper under his arm. Willie eagerly rose from his chair and joined father at his desk

"Here," father said, unrolling drawings of guns he had owned. The two men studied the plans intently. "You may take them with you to look at overnight," father said.

"I'd be honored, sir," Willie said, catching my eye.

When we left the house, Willie tucked the drawings under one arm and held onto his bicycle handlebars with his free hand. "Your father is most generous," Willie said as we walked side by side with our bikes. For a few moments neither of us spoke; then Willie blurted out, "Why must we pretend? You know I care for you."

"I'm married."

"Not very married, I'd say."

"Eddie loves me."

"He loves you, but doesn't make love to you."

I stopped and stared at him. Of course, it was true I was still a virgin although I'd been married a year. Through our many conversations, Willie had guessed as much. "I'd better go now." I bowed my head. "Come to my house for lunch tomorrow. Then we can return father's drawings together."

"We shouldn't see each other too often at your father's. He'll suspect how we feel about each other."

Willie had spoken the words I harbored in my heart.

"Yes," I murmured. "You're right." I looked at Willie's handsome face and saw nothing else. What had I done in marrying Eddie? The future seemed closed off for me.

The following day Willie and I were enjoying a small intimate lunch cooked by Eddie's mother's cook and served by Ah Yuh, when Eddie stormed into the house.

"Willie just dropped by for lunch, wasn't that nice?" I said. "And . . . and it's nice to have you home for lunch, too, Eddie. You've never come home before."

"I changed my mind today," Eddie said, looking pointedly at Willie.

"Ah Yuh, set another place, please," I said. Eddie thumped down in the chair. I looked from one man to the other wondering what might happen.

"You're a student?" Eddie asked with a scowl on his face.

"Yes. Remember, I told you that when we first met."

"You have little time for studying lately, I hear."

"You hear wrong. I study very hard and long. Your wife has been kind enough to introduce me to her father. We share an interest in guns."

"Is that the only interest you share?"

Willie smiled and put down his chopsticks. "I've brought the drawings with me to return to her father today. Ah Tek asked me for lunch since I was coming by anyway. Would you like to see the drawings?"

Eddie didn't answer, but instead pushed his food around his bowl and chewed endlessly on one morsel as if he were unable to swallow.

"Father was delighted to have someone to talk to about guns," I said.

"If you're in engineering, all mechanical things are of interest," Willie added.

"You're interested in many things outside your studies." Eddie's hands curled into fists as he planted his forearms on the table on either side of his soup bowl.

"Ah Yuh, you may take the dishes away." I watched while she whisked away dishes still full of food.

"Would you like fruit?" I asked both men and received grunts, which I interpreted as 'no.' "It was so good of you to come by, Willie, and on such a special day when my husband decided to come home for lunch. Wasn't this an opportune moment?"

Before Eddie could make any accusations, I guided Willie toward the door. "Tell my father I'll see him tomorrow. I have too much to do at home today to come with you."

After I closed the door behind Willie, I felt Eddie's eyes boring into my back, but without a word he left to return to the pharmacy. I wandered into the living room and sat down, thinking of my future. I decided I would continue to see Willie in spite of my marriage.

Two nights later I went dancing with Willie and came home later than usual. As I got out of the pedicab in front of my house, I noticed the glow of a cigarette in our darkened bedroom window. I clutched my jacket tighter, waved good-bye to Willie and watched the pedicab spin away into the dark street.

I walked into our bedroom and turned on the light. Eddie sat glaring at me from his chair across the room. "Where have you been?"

"Dancing with Willie," I shot back, not caring what he thought, and flopped down on the bed.

He rose from his chair in one quick easy motion, moved in front of me and thrust out a picture of Willie that I'd hidden in a locked drawer of my armoire. The conspicuous words, "love and kisses," glared at me from the picture.

"What's this? What's this?" he demanded.

I shook my head and looked away from him.

"For five years I did anything just to be near you and to please you, and you've treated me like a dog. No! If a dog followed you for five years as I have, you'd be nicer to him than you've been to me." He tramped back and forth in front of me, yelling on and on about all he'd done for me.

"Nothing's happened between Willie and me." I said, staring at the floor.

"Nothing but love and kisses!" I lay down on the bed fully clothed and for a while listened to him.

"Where did this come from?" Eddie held up an antique clock Willie had given me.

"What does it matter?" I asked with my eyes closed.

"Did it come from your boyfriend? Don't I give you enough things?"

I kept my eyes shut and heard the drone of his voice coming from a distant place. At two in the morning, I awoke and found him still sitting in his chair watching me. Had he stayed there all those hours? I decided to ignore him, got up, changed into my silk pajamas and went back to bed. He continued to sit there like a dead man. I rolled over and went back to sleep.

When I awoke in the morning, he was gone. Immediately, I called Maria and told her what had happened. Instead of scolding me, she asked how I felt about Eddie's reaction.

"You know what? I feel good. At last he stood up and acted like a man." Was that what I'd wanted? Had I behaved so badly just to see how much Eddie would take? "Can you believe he was sooo jealous of Willie?"

"What did you expect?" Maria said. "Eddie loves you. Be nicer to him."

"I am nice to him, but he's . . . he's just a boy, not a man. I like Willie." I had dreamed of Willie and what it would be like if he made love to me. Even though he and I had hugged and kissed, he'd always remained a gentleman.

"You're playing with fire, Tek. Don't say I didn't warn you. If Mrs. Yong finds out, you'll be in a lot of trouble. After all, Willie was her daughter's boyfriend before you came along."

I hung up and sat pouting. Maria was always warning me as though she were my mother. But I wanted to be loved by Willie.

Maria, however, proved to be right. Mrs. Yong found out I'd been seeing Willie, and that ended my "affair" with him. She spread rumors about me, claiming I'd been chasing Willie, not the reverse. He didn't deny it nor stand up for me. I was furious at his deception, but never regretted the excitement of our romantic time together. Soon Willie was back with Mildred, and he and I stopped seeing each other. But a wedge had been inserted into my marriage and nothing could save it.

Although Eddie continued to try to please me and never mentioned Willie, we still did not consummate our marriage. Now it didn't matter whose fault it was. Week after uneventful week went by without either of us acknowledging our problems or talking about anything of importance. Enough! One evening while Eddie and I sat in our small living room after a quiet dinner, I hurled my final threat at him. "When the war ends, I'm leaving you. Divorce! I must have a divorce as soon as the war ends."

He looked at me with a strange remote expression. Did he think the war would never end? He knew better than I how the war was going; he and his friends had a short wave radio that they listened to in secret. Nothing lasts forever, and even this war would end and with it my ill-conceived marriage.

* * *

In the summer of 1945 after dinner with friends, we returned home, and Eddie immediately shuttered the windows and pulled out his short wave he had stowed behind the couch. "What are you doing?" I asked. "It's late."

"You heard what Jack Chen said tonight. The Americans dropped a huge bomb on Hiroshima."

"That was a few days ago. It doesn't seem to have changed anything."

"Since Germany surrendered in May, the Japanese have no support. Yesterday I learned that Russian troops had attacked the Japanese in Manchuria." Eddie motioned me to come closer and listen to the radio with him. Afraid someone might catch us using the radio, he drew a large comforter over our heads as we sat on the couch together. We listened to the crackling radio for some time without hearing anything new. It was August 9th. Suddenly the clear voice of an announcer said, "The Americans have dropped an atomic bomb on Nagasaki."

I didn't know what an atomic bomb was, but I saw a frightened look in Eddie's eyes. What was this atomic bomb? I listened to the announcer describe the horror it had brought and knew the bomb must be a terrible thing. Could it force the Japanese to surrender?

It was finally over. The Japanese occupation of Shanghai and China ceased. At first we thought the Japanese soldiers would go berserk, pillaging and raping, but near us they were organized and restrained. I heard that the troops turned themselves over to Chiang Kaishek's Nationalist government in preference to being taken by the Communists. The U. S. navy sailed up the Whangpoo and anchored in the harbor. The citizens of Shanghai went crazy; they hugged each other on the street; girls ran up to kiss American officers; men called the officers heroes. Victory parties sprang up everywhere. The Hongkew ghetto dissolved, its inhabitants free to come and go at will.

Soon my friends looked to their futures. Some made plans to join their husbands or families in the States. Others who were going to stay in Shanghai made business arrangements that had been on hold all these years. Willie returned to Hong Kong. My friend Pond left for Canada. Where was my future? Not with Eddie, that I knew.

Our lives in general would now take a better turn or so we dreamed. But victory, instead, brought inflation, unemployment and corruption to the country. When Chiang's son, Ching-kuo, took over the administration of Shanghai, we thought there might be a chance for the city to survive the unemployment and inflation, but that was not to be. Ching-kuo hated the wealthy Chinese and couldn't stop the corruption of his own Nationalist party. Our family was very aware of the growing inflation. Like other businessmen, my father collected yuan from his hotel's nightly take each morning and by the following morning, that same amount bought half of what it had the day before. I'd go to the store with wads of paper money in my purse. By the time I arrived home with an item, its cost would be higher than when I bought it.

A cloud of frustration and discontent lay upon the land, and my life remained an unhappy turmoil as well. Lee Chou came back into my life, and I should have realized that fate was dealing me a hand I shouldn't play.

Chapter 23

"You're seeing Lee," Eddie accused me as we walked into our bedroom.

"That shouldn't surprise you. You and I are going to get a divorce." I flung the words over my shoulder.

Eddie hesitated, turned me around and took my hands in his. His hands were as cold as our marriage. "I beg you, don't leave me." His hands began to shake. "I'll send you to America. You'd like that. You could see the whole world. Just don't leave me."

"It's no good, Eddie," I said, pulling my hands away. "You're good and kind. I'll probably never meet another man as kind as you, but it's no good. I'm not good for you. We just can't make it the way our life is. Tomorrow we'll go to a lawyer and get a divorce. You'll see. It'll be the best thing for both of us."

The following day I made Eddie pick up Maria to be a witness, and we drove around Shanghai until we found a sign indicating a lawyer's office. Once inside, Eddie pretended the whole thing was a joke. I was deadly serious. The lawyer was confused as he listened to me and then listened to Eddie's game playing. Maria stood aside, saying nothing. I knew she would rather be any place in the world than here with us in this small, smelly lawyer's office. No truer friend could I have had.

"There are details to attend to," the fat little lawyer said. "Now..."

"No details," I said. "I just want a divorce."

"I understand, but surely you," he nodded to Eddie, "want to discuss the fine points of the arrangement."

Eddie shook his head. "I'm not interested."

"But surely..."

"All I want," I interrupted, "is a piece of paper saying the marriage is no longer in effect."

The little man was so confused by our behavior that he gave in. "It will cost each of you 5000 *fabi yuan*."

Eddie let out a strained laugh and folded his arms across his chest. "I don't have the money."

Of course he had the money, but I refused to argue with him in front of the lawyer. I opened my purse and gave the lawyer enough money for both of us. He took it and pushed a piece of paper forward for both of us to sign. After Eddie signed, he stood with his back to me, turned and left the office without saying a word. Maria signed as a witness and followed Eddie out the door. I gave the lawyer a fixed smile, picked up the signed papers and walked out of the office; our marriage had ended.

On our way home we dropped off a very silent Maria. After all what could be said? When we got home, Eddie crawled into bed and cried. If he wanted me to feel guilty, he succeeded; yet I couldn't get the picture of a petulant child out of my mind. The next morning in order to make him feel better, I prepared a tray and took breakfast to him. He looked up at me and with tears in his eyes said, "Ah Tek, why can't it always be like this?"

I put the tray on his lap and again felt a surge of guilt.

Why couldn't he understand? "The divorce may be good for one of us, perhaps both of us. If we stay together, we'll both suffer. Someday someone will come along who will love you and be nice to you." I watched his fingers pick at the edge of the sheet. "I can't do that, Eddie."

He reached out for my arm. "I don't care," he said. "You're the only one I'll love until I die."

"You're sweet Eddie."

"Then why, Ah Tek, why?"

"We've been like children playing at marriage. I want more. I want . . ." But I couldn't talk about what I wanted because I didn't want sex with Eddie.

Eddie's last request before I moved out of the house was that the two of us have dinner at the Seventh Heaven, a romantic restaurant on the top of the Park Hotel, where we'd been married. We both dressed up, he in his best suit and I in a green dress and a black suede coat with a silver fox collar. Puzzled by our lack of appetite and by our serious faces, the waiter shot glances at us as he placed the food before us and picked up our barely touched plates. Most of the time Eddie had tears in his eyes.

"Have you told your father?" Eddie asked.

I shook my head. "He'll be angry, but won't say anything. He'll keep his word and stay as your silent partner in the pharmacy."

"I know. He's an honorable man."

"I'll give you ten gold bars and some cash in alimony," Eddie said.

"You don't have to do that."

"I want to. But you're so naïve and innocent about such things, I want you to promise me you'll keep it in a deposit box at the Hong Kong and Shanghai Bank. I'll go with you. Don't let anyone touch it. Use it only for your needs. Promise?"

I nodded, not realizing at the time how prophetic his words were.

After I moved out, I stayed with Maria, because I wasn't comfortable moving back in with my father. She and I filled our days visiting teahouses and going window-shopping whenever she was off work. Days passed with no word from my father. I wasn't surprised he was angry, but I thought I would at least hear from him. After a few weeks of my exile, Auntie Yun arrived at Maria's house. I hurried to welcome her, knowing that she brought word from my father.

I took her hand and led her into the living room. "How's father?" I asked, offering her a chair opposite me.

"Healthy, but sad about your marriage," Auntie Yun said.

I waited for her to say more, but when she didn't, I realized it was up to me to make a conciliatory gesture. "I understand. It will take time to heal his disappointment. I miss not seeing him."

"He feels the same and requests that you move back into his house."

I nodded, for that is what I had hoped she would say. However, moving back into my old room on the third floor would be awkward, for each time I would have to pass Sio Ying's room; yet I had little choice.

The following day I packed up my dowry and moved back into my old room at father's house. Each time I climbed the stairs behind a servant carrying my boxes, I saw Sio Ying's smirking face. I ignored her and continued to move my things into my room. I'd never give her the satisfaction of even acknowledging her presence, but as if she were a dead dragon tied around my neck, I felt the weight of her joy at my new status as a divorced woman. To disguise my feelings, I threw myself into a dating frenzy with Lee.

A month after I had returned to live in my father's house, just when I thought Eddie was out of my life for good, Maria asked me to meet her at a foreign-owned jewelry shop. I met her at the shop's entrance and she led me to the counter. The proprietor had me sit down as he laid before me a jade ring in a diamond setting, a set of onyx and gold earrings with a ring to match and a pair of large gold earrings.

"They're beautiful, Maria, but what's the point? Have you come into some money? You can't afford these, can you?"

"They aren't for me, Tek. They're for you, from Eddie."

"Maria, this is crazy," I whispered to her when the shopkeeper turned to answer a clerk's question. "I can't take such expensive gifts from him. I have no intention of getting close to him again."

"I know. I told him that. I told him you were spoiled, and he was well rid of you, but he wouldn't listen."

I glared at her. "I thought you were my friend."

"I am. No matter how you've treated Eddie, I'll still be a loyal friend. But that doesn't mean I understand you."

"I can't take these gifts."

"He'll lose face if you don't accept something."

She was right. I couldn't walk out without accepting at least one of the gifts. Eddie would lose face. "I'll take the jade ring," I said to the shop owner. "Please return the other pieces to Mr. Lamb."

Out on the sidewalk, I turned to Maria. "Don't ever put me in that position again. I know you mean well for Eddie and me, but nothing will change my mind about restarting a relationship with him."

We walked along the street in silence. She'd been such a good friend for so long, and I knew she was disappointed in me. "I'm going to meet Lee in Hong Kong when he travels there on his next business trip," I told her.

"Tek, you can't! What will your father say? What will everyone say?"

"Lee has arranged for me to stay at a friend's home in Hong Kong while he does business in Canton. Nobody needs to know I'm actually going to be with Lee. I told you, only because you're a dear friend."

Marie thought for a few minutes before saying anything.

Did she know that even I had grave doubts about my impetuous journey?

"If you're set on going, I guess I can't stop you," she said and paused as if she were mulling over what she'd just said. "Well, since you're going anyway, there are things I can't get here on the mainland anymore, like nylons and imported linen. Would you buy a few things for me? I'll give you the money."

I took the three-day boat trip to Hong Kong, and Lee ensconced me at his friends' house. The following day I went on my shopping spree, and later Lee and I went riding in a pedicab down Nathan Road, in Kowloon, the city of nine dragons. Across the bay lay Hong Kong, the harbor of fragrance. It was a wonderful day, the sun shone, and I felt the excitement of the city, or was the throbbing excitement inside me?

Riding with Lee made the day perfect. Suddenly the driver lost control and the cab began to veer on its side. Lee leaped over me and onto the road, unhurt. When the pedicab crashed onto the road, I scraped my cheek on the rough street, and my sunglasses smashed against my face. Blood poured from a cut near my left eye. Lee came over to me, helped me up and dabbed at my bruised face with his handkerchief.

"Did you know it was going to tip over?" I asked, trembling.

"Of course not. But I'm agile. Very light of foot." He laughed.

"But you jumped right over me." I pushed his hand away.

"Tek, don't be a ninny. I had to get out of the way. If I were hurt, how would I be able to help you later?"

His logic in thinking of himself first during the incident should have been a warning to me. Where was my gallant knight?

When I returned to Shanghai with a bandaged eye,

Lucy commented, "Eddie's sister must have put a curse on you."

Could I blame her or his family for thinking ill of me? "And you Lucy, how do you feel toward me?"

"I'm your friend, Ah Tek, not a passerby. I stand by friends."

Did she mean I didn't? I cared how others regarded me, but not enough to dissuade me from being involved with Lee. He was a magnet for me. Yet I remembered that even his friend, Cheng, whom Lee had grown up with, had taken me aside in Hong Kong and said, "For your own sake, don't marry Chou." I believed he was jealous of my taking up Lee's time. Was I not seeing things clearly? It didn't matter. I was drawn to a fate with Lee that nothing could prevent.

Chapter 24

1946–1947

When I returned to Shanghai, instead of worrying about my future, I threw myself into fun and antics. One of my main purchases in Hong Kong had been three of the new transparent raincoats that were the latest fad. During the war plastic of any kind was impossible to get, and I had to pay the equivalent of $80 apiece for the coats. Soon after my return, Maria, her sister and I donned the clear plastic raincoats with their hoods over our heads and paraded down Bubbling Well Road in the rain. We walked past the imposing soaring building of the China United Assurance Society and the small shops next to it with their store fronts full of goods. We giggled at our reflections in the shop windows and felt fashionable despite the sour looks from an elderly couple we passed.

After our fashionable pilgrimage through the city, we stopped in front of Maria's house. "That was so much fun," Maria said. "We weren't as unladylike as those old people thought we were."

"They wanted to make us feel embarrassed," Maria's sister said. "The old people don't realize how much has changed since the war."

"Why would you ever want to spoil all this fun," Maria said, "and run off and marry a fellow like Lee Chou?"

I searched for words. "I can't explain it. He makes me feel . . . alive. How many days will we have like today? I want something out of life. I hate being bored."

Maria said, "If you marry Chou, you'll be a *pei-sai*—a nobody."

I ignored her and everyone else. Even father viewed Lee and my relationship with misgivings, albeit for different reasons. One afternoon as I sat flipping through the newspaper in the living room, I felt father watching me from where he sat. Although I attempted to ignore the power of his silent frown, I eventually had to look up from the paper.

As though he'd been waiting for this opening, he said, "If you marry again, don't get married in Shanghai. Go somewhere else."

His words didn't sound like a wish, but they didn't sound like an order either. I returned my gaze to the newspaper, the words now a blur. I understood the pain I had caused him, but that didn't change my feelings for Lee.

Soon after that conversation, while Lee and I were having dinner in a local restaurant, he said, "Cheng and I are going to Hong Kong the day after tomorrow on business. I've got three tickets on a chartered flight that holds only twenty passengers. Do you want to go?"

"Just like that? Aren't those tickets hard to come by?"

"You bet. But I have connections and I haven't got time to go by boat. We can get married in Hong Kong."

My heart thudded. If I didn't want a boring life, I should take this opportunity. Hong Kong! Adventure! Life with Lee! Everything I'd ever wanted.

On the appointed day, I boarded the plane with Lee. I

had to bend over double to enter the plane to avoid bumping my head and there was no hostess aboard. Inside the DC 3, we passengers sat facing each other on benches lining the sides of the fuselage. But the discomfort didn't bother me. I was going to Hong Kong to marry Lee.

Once in Hong Kong we checked into a hotel. Lee and Cheng shared a room, and I had another small room nearby. We planned to go to the government-run Marriage License Bureau the following day. However, when we inquired about getting registered to marry, we were told that the procedure would take three weeks. Living separately for three weeks in a hotel was out of the question. Instead, we decided to arrange our own marriage ceremony with Lee's friends who lived in the area, sign a certificate and register the document later.

Our first married night was spent in an expensive hotel and sexual union became a reality. Lee's experience in sex made love-making seem exciting, although I wasn't sure what I should be feeling. The following morning I rushed out to a bridal store to rent clothes for our wedding picture—a Western wedding gown, a Chinese style bridal top and skirt, called a *Qui,* and a tuxedo for Lee. Dressed in these clothes, we had our wedding pictures taken in a photography studio. This time my smile was not artificial, but came from the depth of my soul.

For the next three weeks, we entertained Lee's friends in our hotel suite to celebrate our wedding. We remained there for two months, eating out in restaurants or using room service. Lee seemed oblivious to the expense, ordering expensive clothes, having his laundry done by the hotel staff, and tipping generously. He had no idea what a normal, everyday life should be, especially for a married couple. Instead, he was content with hotel living. At times Lee had money and then at other times he seemed to have none. I never connected this phenomenon with some of the unsavory characters Lee visited off and on.

Damage from the war had made housing both expensive and difficult to find. But with the help of Mr. Shen and his girlfriend, Pearl, friends I met through Lee, I found an apartment in Kowloon–a small two-bedroom located on the third floor. We had to pay the equivalent of $5000 just to move in. Lee's friends thought he had money because he entertained lavishly, but I began to learn the truth. It was up to me to furnish the apartment. All my belongings were in storage at my father's in Shanghai, and I had to start from scratch. Mr. Shen and Pearl were my saviors, first finding the apartment and then taking me to inexpensive furniture stores on Shanghai Street for the essentials. Pearl even found Ho Tse (Ho sister), a Cantonese maid, for me. From that time on, Pearl and her Mr. Shen visited Lee and me every weekend.

In time the inevitable pregnancy occurred. I suffered terribly with morning sickness, and our funds were dwindling fast. I wrote to the one person I knew could help me—Lucy. She came to Hong Kong, brought money to me from my safe deposit box in Shanghai and stayed with me through the difficult pregnancy, while Lee continued to travel on business trips. Sometimes he sent money when he was away, but most of the time I had to use my own money for our expenses.

When I went into labor, Lee was in Shanghai. After eighteen painful hours Teresa was born. I remembered Illan's telling me she'd had one foot in the grave when she'd had her baby. Now I understood. Because my labor had been so difficult, for three days after my baby's birth, I had little interest in seeing her. The nuns thought I was a terrible mother and compensated for my indifference by giving the baby extra care.

Lucy and Ho Tse took care of me when I returned home three weeks later. I was so weak from lying in bed that I couldn't even walk. It was Lucy who got up in the middle of the night with the baby and saw to the house chores and my needs as well. Lucy's thin frame grew thinner, until I became worried about her health as well as my own.

When Lee did return two months after Teresa's birth, I thought he would be ecstatic about the baby. He looked at her and smiled. "Cute. She looks like you." He put out his finger and let Teresa grab it, but he never picked her up. Was he just unaccustomed to handling a little baby or unhappy that I hadn't had a boy?

Even before Lee returned, I'd made my decision. "You and I have to talk," I said, pulling him into our living room.

"Don't start on me," Lee said. "It's been a rough business year. I'm doing my best for you and the baby."

"Perhaps, but you're in Shanghai and I'm here. It makes no sense. I intend to return to Shanghai."

"Just like that." He smirked, then smiled. "I can't afford to send you back to Shanghai."

"I don't expect you to. I've booked passage on the President Wilson." He raised his eyebrows. "Don't worry, I paid with my own money."

"Don't you like it here?"

"You're in Shanghai. I'm here. Are we going to have a family life or not? My family, my friends are in Shanghai. I've written father to find a small plot of land where I can build a house. I've always dreamed of owning a house I had built."

He looked at me rather oddly as though this were a strange wish to harbor. Yet I knew deep down inside the reason for this dream. In my mind's eye, I saw myself as a little girl building a wall of bricks the way the workman had shown me when I helped build my father's house. Owning one's own place rather than renting another's was my father's dictum and mine.

"If that's what you want, okay," Lee said. "My prospects in Hong Kong have waned. Perhaps in another year they'll be better. I'll go with you."

And so we prepared to go back to my home—Shanghai. Only Lucy knew how miserable my life had been with my absent, money-spending husband. I would never tell my friends. They'd all warned me. With no plans, no future, and no money, my husband had no alternative but to come back with me to Shanghai. Lee's friend, Cheng, had been right after all.

We sailed on the President Wilson to Shanghai. At my father's home, generous Auntie Yun moved out of her bedroom and gave Lee, my baby and me her room, while she moved into my old small one. Sio Ying stayed out of my way. But her sneer made me grit my teeth each time we passed each other in the house.

When she could utter a word, little Teresa called Auntie Yun, *Mma*, for it was Pun Yun who took care of her from the time she'd cried all night upon our arrival at father's house.

Father had found a small lot for me near his home, and within a year my house was built to my specifications. Because my money had paid for the house and all its furnishings, it was put in my name, not Lee's. Auntie Yun continued to supervise and help take care of Teresa. I naively thought that with this house our lives would take on a semblance of normalcy. But both history and my husband's character made that an impossibility.

It was a Saturday in the winter of 1948. Inflation was skyrocketing. The *fabi yuan* was almost worthless, and the government tried to stop inflation by insisting that we turn in our fabi yuan for a new currency–gold yuan. But the same phenomenon followed that currency. Unemployment remained high, and many were having trouble getting enough food to survive. My father's farmlands were still intact, but the Communists were threatening everyone, and many peasants had turned on their landlords. Still, for the time being we received foodstuff from the land.

One afternoon as I was putting Teresa down for her nap,

Lee came into the room, stared at the baby, then at me. "I'm going back to Hong Kong. I've got business prospects there." He hesitated, then said, "I need money, Tek."

I felt an earthquake of fury shake me, but asked only, "What for?"

"Business. I'll pay you back when I return. Double. I'll pay you back double. You'll see."

My shoulders sagged. My inner voice told me he would never pay me back. But I opened a locked drawer in my armoire and handed him what money I had. He left for a month and returned with the funds depleted. Yet, we continued to live as though money weren't a problem between us.

One night as he and I were getting ready to leave our home for an evening of dining and dancing with friends, our servant let two rough looking men into the living room. These men took Lee aside and spoke in their country dialect, which I didn't understand. One of the men pushed Lee in the chest, punctuating each of his words with a sharp jab. Lee kept giving ground with each push until he was up against the wall. I'd never seen my husband so cowed. I knew without understanding the language that Lee owed them money from gambling in Canton.

After they left, he turned to me with a shrug, his palms upturned. "You see how it is. I need money to pay off a business debt."

"Business debt?" I made no further assertion, avoiding a discussion that could only lead to an argument that would accomplish nothing. I knew he would not or could not change his gambling fever. Denials and excuses could not change the facts. "I'm out of funds," I said. "There's no more cash."

He pointed at the four-carat diamond ring Eddie had given me. Normally I kept it in my jewel case upstairs, but since we were going out, I was wearing it. I covered it up with my other hand. I was stricken with hurt and fear. Had it really come to this?

He must have noticed my alarm. "Forget it then," he said and turned his back on me. After only a moment, he turned back to me again. "Look, I need it! When I make money, I'll get it back for you."

Reluctantly, I slipped it off my finger, knowing full well I would never see it again. What else could I do? To get a divorce again would be unthinkable. I had made myself a cage and with the wrong tiger.

Chapter 25

1950–1952

I was in my home city with my family nearby and I had my own home, a child, but I had a wandering, gambling husband at a time when China was going through political chaos. The Communists were closing in on Shanghai, and people were becoming more desperate. At a family meeting in father's living room, we discussed our options. Each of us dreaded the future, but few of us thought of leaving, except my brother, Shiu Ching.

"We must leave while we can," Shiu Ching pleaded with father. "The Communists can't be stopped. You heard what they've done in the northern part of the country. Taiwan is the place for us."

"I withstood the Japanese and the corruption of the Nationalists," father said. "I can withstand the Communists. After all, they are our own people, not foreign invaders. They wish no harm for the country. They just want us all to share. I don't mind."

Shiu Ching opened his mouth to contradict father, but hesitated.

"My fiancee is here," U-Ching said. "Her family is wealthy and they're staying."

"You'll never be allowed to marry her," Shiu Ching said. "I heard what they want—a five carat diamond ring as your engagement gift to her. You don't have the money to buy it, and I know you can't get it."

U-Ching's eyes narrowed. "Her grandmother likes me. She's going to give me a ring so I can give it to her favorite granddaughter. Then we will marry."

"When the Communists take over, what will you live on?"

"I . . . ."

Father raised his hand to silence the squabble, but he refused to be drawn into their argument. "Our ancestors are here; our future is here. There will be no talk of leaving. The family will remain here."

"Ancestors!" Shiu Ching shouted. "You know what happened to our cemetery in Wu Sih. The Communists decimated it. What does that say for our future, our past? They smashed it to bits." When father said nothing, Shui Ching strode out of the room.

I knew he wanted desperately to leave, for his future in Shanghia looked as bleak as the toppled tombstones of his ancestors. Many of his friends had already left. If he waited much longer, it would be too late, but I doubted he would go against father's wishes. Could any of us leave the land of our ancestors?

Lee was again in Hong Kong, and I had no cash left. I couldn't ask father for money, because he, too, was having a difficult time with inflation. Besides, my pride wouldn't let me ask. Still, I had to do something. One morning I left the baby with Auntie Yun and went to the Hong Kong and Shanghai Bank, where I had stored jewelry. I approached the bank, paused by the two brass lions that guarded each side of the entrance and rubbed the shiny smooth nose of one of the lions for luck, just as thousands of other Chinese passers-by had done.

Inside the vast hall of the bank, my heels clicked on the tiled floor, and for the first time I noticed the echo. I approached the window with my safe deposit key clutched in my hand. The time had come to take my treasures away from their nesting place. Some jewelry had been my mother's, some had come from Eddie. The gold bars of alimony had long since been used to build my house, to feed Lee's habits and to satisfy my needs and my daughter's. I had never told Lee about my horde of jewels. Now even having the jewelry might not help, because there were few people who had money to buy any of the pieces. Still, I would feel safer if the jewels were in my own hands.

I emptied my safe deposit box of jewelry, put the jewelry in my handbag, and gave up the box. It was done. With a heavy heart, I pushed open the bank doors, and as I stepped out onto the sidewalk, I heard someone call, "Tek, Tek." That familiar voice brought tears of joy. It was Eddie. How I had missed his love and tenderness!

He rushed up to me. "It's been a long time. How are you?"

"Fine. And you? I hear you married again and have a child."

He nodded. "You look tired. Let me take you home. I still have my car."

I was so relieved to see a friendly face at my lowest hour that I accepted. The following day chocolate, fruits and Chinese pork sausage were delivered to my home. I knew they were from Eddie. After all this time, he was still trying to take care of me. The food was welcome and I didn't turn it down.

Eddie discovered that I had lunch every day at my father's home and began calling me there, since I didn't have a phone at my home. Soon he was taking me out. This went on for months. It was wonderful to have someone care about me and take me places. I knew our times together made him happy and, therefore, thought there was no harm in our meetings. Delusion often comes from our own needs.

One Sunday he dressed in his Chinese quilted long house gown that he wore only at home, then told his wife he had to check something at the office. Instead, he picked me up, drove out to the countryside, parked his car in the middle of a field and turned off the motor. It was quiet and serene, and for several minutes neither of us spoke.

His gown rustled as he turned to look at me with his sad brown eyes. "Tek, you've broken my heart into pieces. I waited and waited for you to come back to me, but you married Chou. Always remember I'll love you until the day I die." He began to cry.

I put my hand on his arm, for I knew the time for us had passed and it was I who had made this a fact. My eyes stung with tears. "I'll always need your friendship, Eddie. Perhaps you were destined to be my angel."

The car rocked gently and I looked out the car window. Farm children were pressing their noses up against the glass, laughing at the two crying adults inside the car. Eddie started the engine; the children backed away and Eddie drove me home.

Unfortunately, our trip to the countryside had been witnessed by a friend of Eddie's wife. Rumors soon spread that I was chasing Eddie because I had a bad marriage and needed money. Perhaps it was fated that my relationship with Eddie would end in false rumors. He still had me on a pedestal, but I was now forbidden fruit. Eddie had to be erased from my life.

While I struggled through my problems, my brother, U-Ching, lost his fiancee to typhoid. He was devastated.

Before his fiancee died, she had told her grandmother,

"If I live, I want to be one of the Wu family. Please. If I die, I want to be a Wu family spirit."

The grandmother came to U-Ching and asked, "Do you want to marry my granddaughter's spirit?"

In his state of grieving he agreed to marry the spirit of the girl of his desire. To appease him we went along with his marrying the dead girl. It was a strange affair. Candles flickering on a table. His intended's parents sitting in mourning. The grandmother wailing with bereavement for her favorite granddaughter. U-Ching stood and held his fiancée's wooden spirit seat as he declared his wedding vow to her ghost by kowtowing to heaven and earth and to the members of the family, which signified that the Wu family accepted the girl as their daughter-in-law.

While our thoughts were on family matters, the Communists were poised on the outskirts of Shanghai. Now there was more talk of fleeing. A great rush to go south away from the oncoming red tide led to a mass exodus of people following the retreating Chinese Nationalist Army. But for most, time had run out. How was our family to survive once the Communists entered the city? In the past they had brutalized those with money or positions of power. Why would it be different now?

One day after I had lunched with father, I watched him gather documents on his desk. "What are you doing?"

"If the Communists find out I'm a landowner, I'll be in trouble. They've been relentless in the countryside. Poor Lok Hsiao-ming!"

"Why do you say that? What's happened?"

He slammed a paper down on the desk. "It's crazy! How can they do such things? What will happen to the land if the peasants take it over? No organization, no knowledge of agriculture. The food situation will be a disaster. No rice or meat will be coming from the land."

"What's happened to Lok?" I repeated.

He sat down heavily in his chair and put his head in his hands. "Ridiculed. Tortured." He looked up at me. "Must you hear the worst?" He hesitated. "Yes. I see you must. The Communist party members yanked him from his house and forced him to kneel on broken glass with a rope tied around his neck, while those he had hired to work my land threw rocks and spat upon him."

I shuddered, thinking of the chances Lok had taken to bring us food during the occupation. "What about his wife and family?" I knew that after the war with Japan, they'd returned to Wu Sih from Chungking.

"They survived. They live in a small hut and take care of Hsiao-ming's broken body. Others have his house. It makes no sense. He paid them; he was fairer than most land managers."

"What are you doing?" I asked as he lit a match.

"Burning the deeds to the land. I have no choice." He looked up at me with sad eyes and he had never seemed so disheartened. "Perhaps I was wrong. Perhaps you'd better leave Shanghai after all."

I ignored his remark. "What about the deeds to the hotel and the pharmacy?"

"I gave the pharmacy to Eddie after the divorce. The hotel? I'll keep that. We have to have an income and, besides, what would happen to my two hundred employees? They need work; no matter what the Communists do, they understand that people need to work to get paid."

On a metal plate in front of him, the ashes of the deeds curled to black. Much of his life was wrapped up in those small charcoal shreds. What would father's "medicine woman" mother, who had nursed the very same villagers who stoned Lok, think of the world we now lived in?

"The water that carries the boat can also overturn it," he said in a whispered voice.

I sat with him until the sun seeped out of the sky. He said

very little, but there was comfort in our quiet camaraderie. He lit his cigar. "Chiang Kaishek could have pulled our country together. It was easy for him to seize power, but difficult to maintain. I wonder how long these Communists will last?"

Soon after father burned his deeds, the Communists arrived on our doorstep. On April 21, 1949, they crossed the Yangtze River, and our Nationalist troops pulled back. It was the end of the revolution. On May 27, the Communists captured Shanghai, and our lives were changed forever.

At first the changes were felt mostly in the countryside, where the peasants divided up the land and took plots of land for themselves. In cities like Shanghai, newspapers were shut down or taken over by the new order. Courses in Marxism became mandatory.

Rumors of which homeowners would be evicted circulated. Gun Yuen, father's son by Sio Ying, passed father in the street one day and taunted him about his extravagant house. Men dressed in red army uniforms stood by listening intently. The inevitable happened, whether Gun Yuen intended it to happen or not.

Father and his family were ordered out of his house and into a smaller house, where another family already lived on the third floor. Father was allowed to move whatever he wanted, but the house was so small he moved only essentials, like beds, armoires, basic tables, chairs and a sofa. We stood aside while buyers came to look at the beautiful furniture father owned, but no one could afford to buy the expensive wood pieces. Some passed their hands lovingly over the ornately carved wood and shook their heads.

A roughly dressed man came forward. "The only value of these pieces is in the wood itself."

"But look at the quality of the workmanship, the antiquity of the pieces," father said. "Our ancestors spent hours, months, years carving beauty into the wood."

"Not my ancestors, old man. I'll weigh the pieces and

pay you the going price for wood." He turned away from father, then said over his shoulder. "You're lucky the soldiers don't arrest you for hoarding wood."

I watched the buyer weigh the red rosewood desk I'd used for twenty years and the carved chairs and tables that had been in our family since my childhood. Father could only shake his head and turn away. An ache clutched at my chest and it would not leave me until I, too, had to turn and walk away.

The state took over father's house. This meant friends of Mao's now owned what had been my father's property.

Father and his immediate family were allowed to rent the bottom two floors in the small house. When Sio Ying saw that Auntie Yun and my sister Sun Mei would have a room upstairs and that my three brothers would share two rooms, she rebelled.

"I cannot live in such a place," she said to father. "This will never do. I'd have no privacy. I'll find a place of my own to rent nearby."

Sio Ying stayed away from father's house, but he visited her daily. Neither war nor revolution could dim the relationship between father and Sio Ying. Perhaps Gun Yuen had won. After all those years he had succeeded in getting his mother out of Pei Ching's house. He would no longer feel like a turtle.

Chapter 26

Lee and I remained in our small house, and in the winter of 1950, my second daughter, Frances Billan, named after my friend, Illan, and nicknamed BB, was born. This time Lee was present when the baby was delivered at home. Fortunately, it was an easy birth. The following morning snow fell on the city, and we had to use the stove to keep the room warm for the baby. Coal was hard to come by and I worried about the expense.

Shortly after BB's birth, Chou wanted to travel to Hong Kong on business. Again he asked for money, but this time the well was dry. Disgusted, he marched out of the house. Within a short time a new Chou entered my life—Lee's father. He arrived unannounced and expected to be housed with my family and me. His alcoholic breath overpowered me, and I knew he would be trouble; yet I had no choice but to invite the craggy-faced old man to share my meager home. Now I had to deal with the expenses of my children, my maid, Lee's long time office employee, Ah Li, and Lee's father.

Day after day my troubles seemed to mount. I was unable

to nurse the baby and needed to get milk, but I had no cash. I traded a gold chain I had for a one pound can of powdered milk and mixed this with rice powder to appease the baby's hunger.

Life was difficult enough, but the problem of Lee's father's terrible drinking made it worse. Every day the old man sent Ah Li to the liquor store with a big bottle to be filled with strong Chinese rice wine. The old man lived in a constant inebriated state, unable to speak coherently. At times loud slurred yelling came from his room.

One night as my children and I slept, I felt the net cover being pulled from my bed. I looked up and saw the old man standing by my bed, leering at me.

"What are you doing?" I stammered.

"Want to see you and baby," he said in a thick drunken voice.

I jumped out of bed, and pushed him toward the door. "You're drunk, old man. Go to sleep."

He tried to resist, but my shove sent him out through the door. He stumbled, and I slammed the door shut and locked it.

The next morning at father's I told Auntie Yun what had happened. "Ah ya!" she exclaimed. "That animal wants to seduce his daughter-in-law."

"No," I said innocently. "He's just too drunk to know what he's doing."

But that night I locked my bedroom door. Not too long after I'd gone to bed, the doorknob waggled again and again. I could hear him breathing heavily on the other side of the thin wooden door. Finally his shuffling footsteps faded down the hall. After that I began taking the children over to my father's house during the day and having my meals there. Since food was in short supply for them too, my coming for meals was difficult for father and the rest of the family. My problems seemed to be compounding. Ah Li kept asking for money to buy food and liquor for old man Chou. I had only one hope and that was to sell my house.

At this same time, the Communist government wanted huge houses and buildings for office use. The owners didn't want to sell, much less rent, but orders had come down, and the owners had no choice. Now many of these people were looking for smaller places after being forced out of their larger homes. My brother U-Ching found an older couple who needed a smaller place, and my house fit their needs. When they offered me the equivalent of ten gold bars in currency, I accepted.

Now, of course, I had to find another place. Father agreed to have me move into his house and help with the house expenses there. I gave old man Chou money so he could move out of my house and gave Ah Li money to travel back to his home province. But no sooner had I sold my house than Chou's debtors flocked to my door. I paid as many as I could, even though I wasn't sure whether they were lying to me or not about the amounts Chou owed them.

With the sale of my house, my money worries lessened. Life at father's house took on a different tone. Auntie Yun did the housework now that we couldn't afford servants. She cooked for all of us and washed my father's, brothers' and sister's clothes and helped take care of Teresa, who was now a toddler. I had a maid to help with the baby and my small family. I was again content and had reasonable security. Lee stayed in Hong Kong and I never thought about joining him. Shanghai was my home.

In early 1951 terror struck the city's businessmen and capitalists. *Sun Fan Wuh Fan*— the digging out of corrupt, dishonest, wasteful, lazy, tax evading persons—intensified. Workers were expected to point out "suspicious" workers so that they could be interrogated. The "suspect" would be questioned for days and nights and be deprived of sleep. Then exhausted, the person would confess to any "crime," even if he were innocent. During the interrogation, if the official questioner stepped out of the room, it was not unusual for a frantic suspect, guilty or innocent, to jump out of the window. Every day we would hear that someone pegged as a "wrong-doer" had committed suicide. Everyone wondered when it would be his own turn to be investigated.

Of course, we were worried. After all, father employed over two hundred people at his hotel, and although business had fallen off, father was not allowed to fire anyone. Nevertheless, he was expected to pay his employees, even though the hotel had only a few customers. All over Shanghai people were feeling the impact of the Communist presence. We, like others, kept our lights dim at night not only to cut costs but also to avoid drawing attention to ourselves.

One evening as we sat quietly in the small living room under one dim yellow light, our door burst open and five waiters from father's hotel charged into the house. Auntie Yun and I scurried to a corner of the room while father faced them.

"We want our wages," they screamed at father and pounded on the table.

"I have no money to pay you," father said in a steady voice. "No one travels now. You know that. I can't pay you with money I don't have."

"Take out your money!" They shouted at him, saliva spitting out of their mouths.

"I don't have any money," father said calmly.

"You have it. We know. You're a capitalist!"

Father stood before them and said, "I have only my life."

"We don't want your dog's life!" one said.

"Look at your nice furniture and pretty things in the glass cabinets," another said, pointing to the one behind me. "And you say you don't have any money."

"Take whatever you want," father said, waving his hand to include the chairs, tables and cabinet in the room.

That stopped them. They looked at each other, unsure

of their own audacity. Finally their leader said, "You people have a good dinner. Let's have it!"

They barged into the kitchen where our meager meal of leftover rice cooked with salted vegetables and beans sat in pots. Father told them to sit down and nodded to Auntie Yun to feed them. The five waiters wolfed down the food, then stormed out the door.

For the first time I felt our lives were encased by fear. Until now, we'd been fortunate. If there had been any signs of luxurious living in our house, the outcome might have been different. That night fear silenced us.

Finally father turned to me. "Tek Child, this is just the beginning. You should leave for Hong Kong. The rest of the family has little choice, but you might be able to get a permit to visit your husband. It isn't good for you to be mixed up with me."

Despite all that had happened, I refused to listen to his advice. My home was Shanghai, and I vowed to be as pliant as my ancestors had been during their times of political upheaval.

Chapter 27

There was little to celebrate for the Chinese New Year of 1952 during the *San Fan Wuh Fan*. But I wanted to do something to mark the date. I gave Auntie Yun money to buy extra food that would symbolize our new year. I wanted something special so I walked to the market and bought a basket of oranges and a box of Chinese cakes.

Upon my return to my father's house, I noticed a woman dressed in a worn black quilted jacket and pants hovering near the door. I peered at her and slowed my steps. These days threats came from many quarters. When she turned, I was surprised to see Spring Orchid, grandma Zee's *Ya Tua*! Her face lit up, and she rushed forward to greet me.

"No one answered my knock," she said. "I was worried I had the wrong place, but people assured me that this is the house where Wu Pei Ching lives." She darted a look at the house we'd come down to and shook her head. "I thought your father could do something, but now I see he's come to bad luck. I'm not sure he can help me."

"What's wrong?" I asked, gripping my basket tighter. "I'm sure he'll do what he can."

"I don't need help. It's Wong Hai Li and her husband, Yen Tai." She looked from left to right, then lowered her voice. "Can we talk inside?"

I understood her concern. These days we all feared who might misinterpret our actions. I led her into the kitchen. She had changed very little–still thin, still a pock-marked face, yet still a lovely smile. After placing my basket of precious goods on the table, I motioned for her to sit in the straight-backed chair opposite mine and waited for her to explain her visit.

"I should tell your father." She looked around the bare kitchen, then back at me. "Do you live here, too?"

I nodded. "And my two daughters."

"I have three sons," she said with quick pride.

"Father will want to hear what you have to say about the Wongs,"

"No!" She reached across the table and tugged at my sleeve. "Now I see that it's better if I tell you, then you can tell your father, but don't tell anyone else of my visit. I could get into a lot of trouble. My husband would be furious if he knew I had come here. My children could suffer. But I owe your family and Hai Li so much, I felt honor bound to come."

Fear ruled all of us these days. "Tell me about Hai Li. I promise not to tell anyone you were here or that you told me anything." I sat back and waited, but Spring Orchid stammered, unable to begin her story. I urged her on. "We haven't heard anything from the Wongs since the Japanese were defeated."

Hesitantly, she began: "At first Wong Yen Tai was arrested by the Nationalists as a traitor. While he was in jail, he was able to get word to a few influential Nationalists and the American military and he convinced them he'd been forced against his will to work for the Japanese."

"From what I'd heard that's possible. It was Yen Tai's

association with the Japanese that saved father from arrest at the Hongkew Garden Bridge."

"I don't know what's true, but I heard the Nationalists released Yen Tai and offered him a position in the Central Financial Institute as a legal consultant," she said. "When the Communists took over, they interrogated him and for a while he worked for them. But now he's branded a traitor, and they've arrested him again. I can't find out what's happened to Hai Li."

"Do you know where she lives?" I asked, wondering what father could possibly do.

"I have her address, but I'm afraid to visit her. Can you find out what happened to her?"

I didn't want to let Spring Orchid know that my fear of the Communists was just as strong as her fear. Of course, Yen Tai's rescuing father at the bridge was a debt that should be paid. Besides, I had always liked Hai Li, for she had treated me as an intelligent adult when I was only a teenager.

Although I knew father would help if he could, he was in a difficult position. His trouble with the authorities over his hotel was a mark against him. Another clash might put him in jail. I took the Wongs' address from Spring Orchid and told her I'd do what I could. She accepted my pledge and hurried from the house, not looking back once she gained the street.

There was plenty of light left in the day, and the maid was looking after the children. I realized that it was up to me to meet our family obligation. It was better that I go alone to the Wongs and not bring a friend. What harm would it do to visit Mrs. Wong? I'd bring the basket of oranges along as pretext for my visit.

I hurried along the streets trying to look inconspicuous. The Shanghai address was in a modest section provided by the Communist Central Financial Institution. I knocked sharply on their door. When there was no answer, I rapped louder. The next door neighbor peered out her half-opened door to see what was going on.

"Sorry to bother you," I said. "Do you know where Wong Hai Li is?"

Fear flickered in the woman's eyes. "I don't know. Not my affair." Before she pulled back into her house, she said, "Try the Red Cross Hospital."

"What's wrong with her?"

The woman shook her head and waved me away. Without another word she shut her door, preventing the world from creeping into her life. How long had I been like her?

Without thinking of the consequences for myself, I rushed to the hospital. It took me a while to find Hai Li, but eventually I found her in a third class ward. At first neither of us recognized the other. She had been petite, smooth of skin and keen of wit. Now she was old and withered, like an olive left to rot on the ground. She peered at me through watery eyes, then smiled in delight.

"Tek Child," she said. "Are you surprised I know you?"

"It's been a long time," I said, standing by her bed.

Her weak voice trembled. "I've followed your family through the years. I never forgot how your father made his home our home. Yen Tai had ambition, but in the end, he hadn't forgotten either."

"I know." I patted her gnarled hand that lay inert against the white sheet.

Suddenly tears poured down Hai Li's old face. "I didn't do anything wrong. I'm innocent!"

She struggled to sit upright in the hard bed. "Come closer," she beckoned me.

I moved to the head of her bed. For a moment I thought she'd lost her sanity. But as her words streamed out like a pot about to boil over, I knew she needed to spill her story into my open heart and ears.

"I'm innocent. Really." She clung to my hand. "I just did

what Mrs. Sun asked me to do for her. I kept eight gold bars for her. She didn't want her husband to get them. I returned them to her. I don't want trouble. It wasn't my fault. That's all there is to it. I didn't want to get involved. They want names. They want me to confess that I hid other people's money, too."

I knew the "they" she referred to were the Communists. Despite her weakened condition, she gripped my arm so tightly I could feel her fingernails biting into my flesh.

"I was so frightened. I tried to name some people. You know I don't have many friends here. I even thought of you. I almost mentioned your name."

My hands went cold and a steel vise clamped over my heart. I glanced around the crowded ward at the faces turned our way and I knew ears were listening for any detail that might help others get on the good side of the Communist authorities. If I reasoned with her, I might make things sound worse.

"Poor thing," I said, raising my voice. "You must tell the truth, no matter what. But you should never say anything that isn't true." Would that satisfy the big ears in range of our conversation? "How did you end up in this hospital?"

"I'm not sure. I remember they came to my house to question me. They took me from my house. I wore only my nightgown. They put me into this ward."

Wanting to ease her misery, I told her, "I'll bring you clothes tomorrow."

She didn't seem to have heard me. Her hands fluttered. "I remember. I remember. When they came to question me about Mrs. Sun, I swallowed broken glass and pins." She glared at me defiantly as though I were the enemy. Her gaze flitted from bed to bed. Suddenly she covered her mouth with both hands, obviously afraid of who might hear such a confession.

The next day I gathered up a quilted silk wool long gown, a sweater, some underwear, woolen socks and warm slippers and returned to the hospital. On the way I passed a street vendor selling hot chestnuts. I recalled how much Hai Li had enjoyed chestnuts and bought a warm bag for her.

When I arrived at the hospital, Hai Li greeted me effusively with tears in her eyes. "You're the only one who comes to visit me. Where's my husband? Where are my friends?" She tore open the bag of chestnuts and nibbled on the sweet meats like a squirrel. "I'm in Shanghai, aren't I? That's why no one comes to visit."

I sat down at the edge of her bed and again listened as she poured forth her tale.

"After the Nationalists fled, Yen Tai worked for the Communists at the financial institution. He came home every night tired of the endless interrogations conducted in his office by a Communist officer." She raised her finger to her mouth. "I must talk softly. They have Yen Tai now somewhere. They hauled him off to prison just like the other workers. They force everyone to confess to crimes they haven't committed. Sometimes men would implicate others. There was nothing I could do, nothing he could do. He had nothing to hide. We had no money hidden. When he told me that poor Mr. Sun had been arrested and interrogated because they believed he had money, I confessed to Yen Tai about the gold bars Mrs. Sun had given me."

Hai Li rocked back and forth, hugging her arms tightly to her chest. "What could I do? I had to tell my husband what I'd done for Mrs. Sun. Yen Tai shouted at me: 'God! What have you done? How could you be so stupid? Now I must confess this first thing tomorrow morning. I'm in terrible trouble.'

"That night neither of us could sleep. We were in great danger because of my stupidity. We talked it over and agreed that Yen Tai would go to Communist headquarters and confess what I had done. In the meantime, I would return the gold bars to Mrs. Sun."

Hai Li shook her head back and forth. "No matter. No matter. When I returned home from Mrs. Sun's two men and a woman were waiting for me on my doorstep. They pushed me into my house even after I tried to explain that I'd returned the gold bars to Mrs. Sun. They had such stern looking blank faces. I was so scared. They said they'd sent officers to arrest Mrs. Sun. They pointed their fingers at me and said I must have kept American money and jewelry for Mrs. Sun too. I kept telling them this wasn't so, but they wouldn't believe me. They wouldn't believe me!"

Abruptly, Hai Li stopped talking. She stared out into the dim light of the ward. I hadn't said a word and simply waited for her to continue.

"They searched my house, but they couldn't find anything. We had nothing left except Yen Tai's books. They confiscated his books and my jade ring and earrings, and my gold wedding band. But this wasn't enough. They kept yelling at me to confess. Confess what? I was innocent.

"I was so scared I wet my pants. Disgraceful! I had to use the toilet." She grabbed my jacket, pulled me closer and whispered, "I found pins in the bathroom and swallowed them and tried to force pieces of broken glass down my throat. They heard. They broke into the bathroom and found me covered with blood. They thought I was out of my mind and brought me to this place."

She must have been out of her mind with fear. After she was talked out, I left, promising to return soon. The authorities' terror tactics had made this educated, refined woman so deranged that she had mutilated herself. It was beyond my understanding, but so many such tales had been told throughout Shanghai that I didn't doubt her story.

Two days later as I was leaving the house to visit Hai Li again, the phone rang. I was alone at the time. Auntie Yun had taken the children out, and father had been called to the hotel. The man on the other end of the line spoke with authority without identifying himself. But I knew it had to be the police.

"We want to question you about your visits to Mrs. Wong," the voice growled. "You will come to the Communist police office downtown!"

Shaking, I hung up the phone. I had to go. There was no avoiding the order. I called Lucy.

After listening to my trouble, she said, "I have a friend whose husband works at the United Nation's office downtown. I'll call her, then I'll go downtown with you and wait in her husband's office for you.

"You must tell father what's happened to me in case I don't come back."

"I can hear the panic in your voice. I'll be at your house as soon as I can."

Chapter 28

The minute Lucy arrived, we hailed a pedicab to take us downtown. As we rode, Lucy tried to reassure me. "Don't worry. You've done nothing wrong. I'll wait for you at the United Nation's office no matter how late it is."

I thought of Hai Li's experience and felt my knees ache with weakness. Why had I gotten involved? The whole matter was none of my affair, or was it? How could I have not reached out to Hai Li? What kind of people had we become if we couldn't help each other?

The pedicab stopped in front of a large nondescript office building. I hesitated, then stepped out of the pedicab. "Good bye," I whispered to Lucy.

"It'll be all right," she said. "Just remember you've done nothing wrong."

I took a deep breath and walked inside the building down a long dimly lit hall papered on both sides with signs blaring out slogans. "Down with Capitalism! Beat down the evil enemy America! Glory to Mao!"

This slogan-slathered hall yawned before me like a gaping mouth from hell. With hesitant steps, I walked down the long corridor, clutching the slip of paper with the room number as though it were my ticket to safety instead of my ticket to interrogation and perhaps my doom.

At the end of the hall, I found the room. A man in a drab-colored uniform slouching against the doorjamb stared at me. I gave him my name. "I was asked to come to this office," I said.

Without a change of expression, he pointed toward a stool sitting outside the room. "Wait there!"

I felt the tension in my stomach as I waited, sitting on the stool. From time to time I asked the guard questions, but he looked past me as if I weren't even there. Time ticked by and with each passing moment, my apprehension rose. After an hour the door jerked open and a man waved me into a huge room. A large empty conference table sat like a squat bug in the middle of the room, with one chair nudged up against it. At the far end of the room stood another long table with several men sitting behind it. The man who had beckoned me into the room ordered me to sit at the lone chair at the conference table. Then he left, closing the door to my freedom behind him.

Again I waited. The men at the far end of the room ignored me and talked amongst themselves, looking in my direction from time to time. It was all part of the game. I can play this game, I told myself. I will be calm, cool, reserved. After another half an hour, one of the men rose and walked toward me. He was tall and handsome. "I am Comrade Woo." He pulled up another chair, flipped its back away from him, straddled it and sat facing me.

"You and Mrs. Wong are good friends," he began as if he knew me. Then his tone changed. "You knew she was involved in a conspiracy with Mrs. Sun to hoard money. Mrs. Wong has confessed she gave you American money and you hid it for her."

I jumped to my feet, forgetting my vow to keep a cool

head. "That's not true. I went to her house to visit her for the Chinese New Year. I hadn't seen her for years. Why would she have given me money? We weren't that close."

"Then why did you visit her?"

"I heard she was ill." Trembling, I sat down again.

"If you aren't that close a friend, why is it you are the only one to visit her in the hospital? You brought her food and clothes."

"I went because she's a nice lady and there was no one else to help her. I did what a friend should do." I tried to measure my words, but I was angry as well as scared.

"What's your opinion of Mr. and Mrs. Wong?"

"They are a decent, honest couple. I took her food because she couldn't afford to buy sugar or chestnuts. I felt sorry for her. She and her husband live on what they earn. They have no other money." Was this true? Had Yen Tai gotten rich under the Japanese and then lost his wealth? If he had, what happened to their money when he was in prison?

Comrade Woo looked me up and down as though I were a foreign object. "At one time Mrs. Wong was rich. When she became poor, she became greedy. She must have gold or money at other friends' places. She said she left four thousand dollars at your house."

"No! No such thing happened. You're just making that up."

"We know that it did happen," Comrade Woo shouted. His voice grew louder with every word. "You've hidden money. You're involved. You're trying to take money from the people!"

I continued to deny all his accusations. The arguing and shouting went on and on without an end in sight. Suddenly, a big heavy-set man rose from the long table where he had been listening with the other men and moved behind me. He banged his fist down on the table in front of me, put his face near mine and sneered. "You're a real tiger." He plucked at my leopard skin coat. "You need to be taught a lesson."

I stared at the far window to avoid looking at him and understood why people had attempted to escape any way they could. These men didn't want to hear the truth. I needed to find another tack, because what I had been doing up till now hadn't helped. The water that drives the boat can also overturn the boat, my father had said. Yes! That was the answer.

Comrade Woo again took over questioning me and as he ranted on and on, I stopped trying to counter every one of his statements. I rode with the flow of his accusation. I entered an inner state of calm as if I were being transported to an eddy out of a rumbling river. When Comrade Woo finally ran out of things to accuse me of, I made my statement in a language they could understand.

"Comrade Woo, you have convinced me. I will cooperate with you. If I find out anything about Mrs. Wong or her husband, I will notify you at once."

"Now you have the right attitude." He puffed out his chest and nodded to his comrades at the far table.

"May I leave now?" I asked.

He peered at me through narrowed eyes. "Yes, but remember, any time we need you, you must come immediately."

They thought they'd won, and that's what they had to continue to think. "I'm at your disposal." I walked stiff-legged down the hall of hell, stumbled out of the building and found a pedicab to take me to the United Nation's office, where Lucy and her friend's husband waited for me. It was late, past closing time, but they had waited. When I walked into the office and saw familiar faces, I choked up and sobbed wildly.

Back in my father's house, I worried day and night that "they" would call me again. I had told my family of my ordeal and all of us were tuned to a nervous pitch of anticipation. Whenever the phone rang, we cringed.

While I had my ordeal with Comrade Woo, father had been badgered by other officials to turn over his hotel to the state. "We will be partners," the official told him. "You and the state will work together to make the hotel prosperous." Father knew this meant the state would take over the hotel and there was little he could do about it. The income was gone; the land and building were worthless because no one traveled any more. Father's business world had collapsed. He no longer had money, but the Communists still considered him a capitalist.

After a week I began to think that the officials had forgotten me, but a phone call from Wong Yen Tai dispelled that notion. Although I hadn't spoken to him in years, I could tell his voice was stiff, unnatural and flat. This was not the confident man I once knew. Had they destroyed his character?

"Let me have three ounces of gold," he said over the phone. "I need it."

"I don't know what you're talking about," I said. "I don't have any gold."

"I need it urgently."

"I'm sorry, but I don't have it."

He hung up without another word. Had I done the right thing? Did he really need money or was he being forced to try to incriminate me? After my experience at the Communist police office, I didn't know whom to believe any more. Had I caused the Wong's more trouble? Would this be the beginning of more trouble for my family or me? I had to wait for answers, and in the meantime my head was heavy with the weight of Communist intrusion into our lives. China no longer felt like home.

I had hoped the phone calls would end. I had little choice but to stop visiting Hai Li in the hospital. My family could suffer. The Communists counted on fear. We were a nation forced into the throes of paranoia about our families and our friends.

Another phone call came, but this time U-Ching was in the house with me as well as Auntie Yun. I listened apprehensively as Wong Yen Tai asked me again for money, but this time his voice sounded sincere.

"I'm at the hospital visiting my wife. It's time to check her out, but I don't have the money to pay the hospital. Could you please lend me the money so we can leave?"

"I'd like to help you," I said, "but I don't want any more trouble."

"I'm through with my ordeal with the authorities," he said. "I've been exonerated. They released me. Last time I called you they told me what to say, but now I'm calling for my wife and myself. Please help. I wouldn't ask if I had another choice."

I hung up without promising him I would come. I still had doubts about getting involved with the Wongs again. U-Ching and I discussed the matter and finally agreed that we would go together and see if they really did need help. On the way to the hospital I stopped and bought small Chinese cakes and fruit for the Wongs. If the call had been a ruse, we could say we were only bringing food to cheer the patient.

With cautious steps, U-Ching and I walked into Hia Li's room. For a moment I didn't recognize Yen Tai. I remembered him as a tall, slim erect man with an assured manner. Now his stooped shoulders and thin neck supported his swollen face and he looked at me with tired eyes. He stood by his wife's bed. A doctor faced him on the other side of the bed.

After the Wongs' welcomed us with smiles, the doctor prepared to leave.

"Please don't leave," I said to the doctor. "I've come here to help Mr. Wong pay the hospital bill and for nothing else." The doctor smiled pleasantly, but looked puzzled. "The first time I came I had just learned that Mrs. Wong was here," I continued, lowering my voice. "I simply came to visit her as a friend should do. Then I was accused of conspiring with her and was called in and interrogated by the authorities."

The doctor held up his hand and gave me a sympathetic smile. "I understand. I'll stay. You have nothing to fear. There'll be no problem with this."

In front of the doctor and a nurse, U-Ching and I pulled out a small sum of money to settle the account. I gave Hai Li the basket of fruit and cakes and wished her and Yen Tai well. I had no intention of seeing them again.

Once my brother and I left the hospital, I breathed a sigh of temporary relief. But the sense of terror stayed with me. Along the street, hazy sunlight filtered through the windows of the old English style concrete buildings, and I marveled at the vacant streets, formerly bustling with activity. This is what Communism had done. Destroyed the heart of the great city of Shanghai; destroyed the soul of its people. Now I would always have doubts about my safety as well as my family's. It was time for me to leave China. The bigger question was how?

Chapter 29

1952

The evening meal of rice and vegetables had been cleared away and baby BB was already in bed. Teresa, my toddler, held her arms up to her Auntie Yun, crying "Wai-boo, Wai-boo, story time, please, please, Wai-boo."

Auntie Yun picked Teresa up in her loving arms and took her off to bed. It was a nightly ritual both Teresa and Auntie enjoyed. Could I take my child away from such love?

The yellow glow from the one living room lamp seeped across the worn carpet. I was as tense as the rigid wood-backed chair I occupied. Father sat in his usual flower-print-covered upholstered chair. U-Ching stood on the far side of the room, smoking, and Shiu Ching slouched on the sofa. The family knew of my intention of finding a way out of China and none had tried to dissuade me from leaving.

"I've found a way to get permission to obtain exit permits for myself and the children to visit Hong Kong," I began. My father and brothers nodded and waited for my explanation.

"Lucy's in Hong Kong now. She'll write a letter to me telling about Lee's affair with a dance hall girl." I raised my hand and shook my head at their stern looks. "It isn't true, but I need a ruse. I must make the authorities believe I'm taking my children to Hong Kong to force my husband's return so the four of us can be together as a family here in China. It's the only way they'll let me take the children with me."

"Is there no other way besides lying?" father asked. "The *San Fan Wuh Fan* movement has died down."

"That's why people are trying to flee," Shiu Ching said. "Now is the opportunity before the government thinks up some new trick to enslave us."

"I haven't been able to come up with another plan," I said.

"If you get out, what will you live on?" Shiu Ching asked. "Lee hasn't been a good provider in the past. Can you depend upon him?"

"No, I can't." This had been my worry as well. But I still had money left from the sale of my house.

"The authorities will let you take out only ten yuan, one ounce of gold, and twenty ounces of silver," U-Ching said.

"What about jewelry?" I asked him.

"Only what you wear and that better not be too much or they'll confiscate it." He crushed his cigarette in an ashtray.

"She can take clothing or material and household goods," Shiu Ching said, moving forward to the edge of the couch, fully involved with making plans. I knew he would leave too if he could find a way out.

"I'll have my old tailor make many different cheongsams," I continued. "That way I won't have to buy anything for a long time."

"You can sell some of your goods if you need money," Shiu Ching said.

"There has to be a way to hide some of my jewelry." Now I became convinced my plan would come to fruition.

U-Ching smiled and nodded. "I'll help you with the details when the time comes. Perhaps I can make contacts in the black market to get American dollars."

I looked to father for his reaction to my plan. His face was blank, but there was no disapproval, only the gaze of a man who knew his life had come unraveled and there was little he could do to stop the thread from being pulled.

The following day I began shopping. I bought silk, wool and cotton to be made into cheongsams for my girls and myself. Even at that tense time, I cared about my appearance. Besides, I justified my shopping spree as an investment in my children's and my future.

For forty years cheongsams had remained fashionable. Only slight changes had been made—the length of the hem and the sleeves, the width of the collars, or the length of the side slits in the gown. When the tailor came to the house for the material, I explained to him what kind and color lining as well as the type of frogs (hand made buttons) I wanted. A Chinese woman of means would never buy a ready-made cheongsam. I had my tailor make twenty cheongsams.

I made my next purchase from a tailor who sewed nothing but Western dresses, coats and jackets. He brought a fashion magazine to the house from which I picked out styles for woolen jackets to match my woolen cheongsams. I also had him make a few lightweight woolen coats for Hong Kong's mild climate.

My clothing taken care of, next I visited a famous shoe store–*Comfort*–which made shoes to their client's measurements. I ordered several pairs of shoes for myself and bought three pairs of imported children's shoes in different sizes for each of the girls.

For two months I shopped, preparing for my Hong Kong trip. I gradually filled the two camphor wood chests that I would take through Customs and ship to Hong Kong. I was not alone in this endeavor. Many other people were also making plans to leave for Hong Kong, our only allowable destination. The stores had an unusual, although temporary, boom in business. Tailors all over the city were swamped. However, since other countries weren't trading with China, stores' stocks dwindled and without re-supplies, many eventually had to shut down.

When I received a notice from the Public Security Bureau in our area to come for an interview, I was ready. I had a photo of myself with my two children and round trip tickets to Kwong Chon (Canton). After a surprisingly brief interview, I was told to be ready to leave in two weeks and was given an exit and a re-entry permit. I was told to take my packed chests to an appointed warehouse.

Even though I now knew I could leave, I still had much to do. Father gave me the name of a friend of his who would trade Chinese currency for $100 American bills. Once I had these bills, I rolled them inside a wooden frame then sewed the frame onto my handbag. I went to the China Bank where they issued me a certificate allowing me to leave with my gold chain, which would be the one ounce of gold I was allowed to take out of the country. The permitted 20 ounces of silver I took in the form of ten silver dishes from a set I'd received when I'd first married Eddie. The remaining dishes I sold to the bank for the value of their weight. U-Ching helped me buy a few gold coins through the black market. I sewed the gold coins I received from these various transaction into my bra.

Before I closed my camphor chests of clothes and kitchen goods, I wrapped a few pieces of jewelry in paper and stuffed the paper inside a teapot already in the chest. With misgivings, I sent the chests off to the assigned warehouse, where they would be inspected before shipment. Later with my brother U-Ching accompanying me, I went to the same warehouse to see if my chests would pass inspection. If they found contraband, what would happen to me?

"Everything will be all right," U-Ching said, noticing the perspiration on my forehead.

"I hope so." I clutched my handkerchief. I didn't dare tell him I had hidden a jade and diamond ring inside my handkerchief. I intended to smuggle the ring into my chests after they'd been inspected.

When we arrived outside the warehouse, guards waited at the entrance to scrutinize all those who were going to go inside. "Leave your purse there," a guard said, pointing to a desk.

I smiled, nodding my willingness to conform, but my body felt as if it were on fire. I put my purse down on the table, hoping they'd be more interested in it than in me. While guards searched U-Ching and me from head to toe, another guard emptied my purse. As the guard patted me down to see what I might be hiding, I raised my arms and dabbed at my face with my handkerchief. Apparently the guards were used to nervous customers and regarded my agitation as natural behavior.

After the guards were satisfied we weren't hiding any contraband, I was allowed to scoop up the contents of my handbag and dump them back into it. All the while I kept my handkerchief clutched in my hand. We were then directed into a cavernous warehouse piled high with luggage waiting to be shipped. U-Ching and I had to search for my two chests, separate them from the rest of the stacked boxes and chests and open them for inspection by a Custom's officer.

He strolled over and poked about the top layer of goods in the chests. I had packed the children's clothing and kitchenware on the top. He looked at me and smiled. His stick lingered on the teapot. "It's fine. You can close them now."

Before closing the lid on one of the chests, I leaned over it, pretending to put things in order and at the same time threw my handkerchief with the ring into the chest. Once I had locked both chests, the officer marked them with chalk, indicating they were ready for shipment. I thanked him, and U-Ching and I left the warehouse.

Slowly, painfully each step brought me closer to my goal of leaving China.

A week before my hoped-for departure while the family sat outside in the yard after dinner on a warm evening, the Wongs paid us a surprise visit. I greeted them with pleasure even though they were the reason for my frightening experience with the authorities and my subsequent decision to leave China. Through them I had learned that getting involved in other people's problems could result in terrible personal consequences. Would I have done otherwise if I'd known what the result would be? No! I couldn't deny the sufferings of friends.

It was the first time father had seen Yen Tai since the encounter on the bridge during the Japanese occupation. At first they were stiffly cordial to each other, but as the visit lengthened, father's warmth toward his old friend resurfaced. With my immanent departure, I was delighted that father's friendship with Yen Tai might be renewed. If this could happen, it would prove that friendship can withstand the tide of history.

Auntie Yun brought out bowls of sweet green bean soup, a summer time drink that had a cooling affect. As Hai Li sipped from her cup, I thought of how she had looked in the hospital. Now although still frail from her ordeal, her petite frame was once again straight, her eyes clear, and her keen intellect reborn.

"We heard you were leaving," she said to me. "I had to come to see you one more time and thank you for your help."

I was going to ask her how she'd learned of my coming departure, but father interrupted. "You both survived a terrible experience. Yen Tai, all your education couldn't prevent what happened to you. Is China doomed?"

"Everyone pushes a falling fence," Yen Tai said. "For now we must wait. We must endure. Times change. You've seen this in your lifetime. We are all little birds waiting for summer. Unfortunately we are now in winter." He settled back in his chair and looked at my children who were playing at the far end of the yard. "It's good you take your children away, Tek. Remember China and come back home again some day."

"Tell us of your time in prison," U-Ching said, obviously trying to avoid a maudlin scene over my coming departure.

Our family was silent as we leaned forward to listen to Yen Tai's tale.

"Do you know how much we need our sleep? The most terrifying part of my confinement was not the interrogation, but the lack of sleep. I'd have said anything just to be allowed to sleep. But they didn't want a confession out of desperation, they wanted their 'truth.' In the middle of the night soldiers came and yanked twelve of us out of the building where we'd been held and transferred us in a prison van to a house. I have no idea of its location. We were told we were going to a place where we could think about our false confessions.

"This house had many rooms. In each room ten of us were kept under constant guard. During the day we had to sit motionless in a chair, focusing our eyes on one spot in the room. We weren't allowed to talk or move unless given permission. If we had to cough or scratch, we had to raise our hands and get an okay to do so. At night I wasn't allowed to turn over in my bed unless the guard said I could. We were puppets controlled by the guards."

His mouth turned upward slightly. What could possible be amusing? I remembered my own interrogation and thought only of the terror it had instilled in me.

"One day the lights failed in our room," Yen Tai continued, "and the guards had to call in an electrician. When the poor man came in and saw ten motionless men staring at nothing, he began to tremble. With shaking hands he finished working on the wires, then dashed out of the room as if it were filled with ghosts. It's amazing what you can see with your peripheral vision."

Although we smiled at his story, I'm sure my family shared my relief that we hadn't endured such mindless treatment.

"There was one good thing that came of my incarceration." He sipped his cup of soup, then put it down on the grass by his chair. "You will forgive my speaking of such a matter." He nodded to Auntie Yun and me. "But we must find something good out of horror. At a given time every day we were lined up to use the bathroom, whether we needed to or not. As each of us entered the toilet area, a soldier at the door pointed his rifle at us, shouting, 'Hurry, hurry, hurry!'" Yen Tai laughed. "Those three months of imprisonment cleared up my constipation. Before, I needed to sit and concentrate for an hour or so. Now I'm in and out of the bathroom in two minutes."

Self-consciously we joined in his laughter but soon relaxed and talked of family matters. BB crawled up onto my lap and Teresa cuddled in Auntie Yun's arms. The night ebbed, and the Wongs took their leave. I watched Yen Tai and father walk side by side to the gate with their heads together, talking as they had done so many years before in my father's compound at our old house. Tears welled up in my eyes. My days of seeing such sights were numbered.

On August 15, 1952, my two baby girls and I were ready to leave. Auntie Yun prepared breakfast for us, but Teresa just sat at the table crying and refusing to eat. "I want to stay with Wai-boo," she complained. "I want to stay with Wai-boo!" There was no appeasing her.

Should I leave her behind? I looked at BB, who was excited about the train trip. The coming changes in her life were meaningless to her. I left the two children and Auntie Yun in the kitchen and went to father's room. He stood silhouetted against the window, his head lowered as he gazed out into the daylight.

"We're leaving now." I stood there with my arms at my side unable to find words. "Please take care of yourself." A string of emotion stretched between us as unseen as a spider's thread, but as strong as a rope.

He half turned, but didn't raise his head. "Take care of yourself and . . . and Tek Child, Tiger . . . write."

I turned away. Words, caught somewhere between my mind and my lips, were left unsaid. The diesel-fueled taxi U-Ching had arranged to take us to the train station waited while he and Shui Ching stowed my luggage in the cab. Then Shiu Ching carried a screaming Teresa out to the street and placed her beside me. Once inside the cab, I held BB on my lap and tried to control Teresa's outrage. I looked back at Auntie Yun, who stood stiffly waving from the gate, wiping away the tears that streamed down her face. Teresa banged against the back window with both hands, crying, "I don't want to go!" as the cab drove off.

I was leaving Shanghai, a magnificent city I had fallen in love with the very first time I arrived and paraded down its pulsing, crowded streets in a broad blue sash that I'd coerced my mother into buying for me. I'd strutted like a bird without a cage. For years China and Shanghai had been my home, but it had become a prison. I clutched my children to me, knowing I was protecting them from the horror of what China had become.

At North Station we boarded the train to Canton. Through tears born of regret and love, I watched the city of Shanghai pass by and fade from view.

Epilogue

Wu Tek Ying changed her name to Alma Wu when she emigrated with her daughter, Frances Billan (BB), to the United States in 1967. Her first-born daughter, Teresa, died in Hong Kong in 1963. Alma Wu is now a United States citizen.

Wu Pei Ching, Tek Ying's father, died in 1968 at home of a heart attack before Pun Yun could get him to the hospital. Alma heard of his death six months later from her friend Lucy, who continued to live in Hong Kong. Alma never let her father know she had immigrated to the United States for fear of the punishment he would have incurred if the Communists learned he had a daughter in the United States.

Pun Yun died in 1971 from food poisoning. She had been taking care of her grandchildren by her second son, Tsu Ching, as well as Sun Mei's children. Tsu Ching died in 1984. Sun Mei still lives in Shanghai.

Sio Ying died in 1956 of an internal infection.

U-Ching stayed faithful to his ghost bride and never remarried. He died in 1983 in Shanghai.

Shiu Ching came to the United States in 1984 and after thirteen years returned to Shanghai.

Wong Yen Tai died in a Communist prison camp in Beijing.

Alma's daughter, Frances Billan, lives in the United States and graduated from UCLA and is currently in the medical device industry in southern California. She has one daughter, Candice, a graduate of UCLA who attends Loyola Law School.

Alma's son, Andrew, born in Hong Kong in 1957 graduated from UCLA with two Master's degrees. Currently, he is an executive in the banking industry in Shanghai. He is the father of twin boys, Christopher and William.

Tek Ying's second husband's name is fictitious.

OLD AND NEW SPELLINGS

Throughout the book we have used the old spelling of words in keeping with the historical time frame of the story. The following is a list of the old and new spellings and name changes made under the present government of The People's Republic of China.

OLD	NEW
Wu Sih	Wuxi
Whangpoo River	Huangpu River
Hongkew	Hongkou
Nanking road	Nanjiing Lu
Shantung Province	Shandong Province
The Bund	Zhongshan Dong Yi Lu
Cathay Theatre	Guotai Theatre